The Puffin Book of

Funny Stories

CHOSEN BY

HELEN CRESSWELL

Illustrated by Ainslie MacLeod

PUFFIN BOOKS

PUFFIN BOOKS

Published by Penguin Group
Penguin Books Ltd, 27 Wrights Lane, London w8 5tz, England
Penguin Books USA Inc., 375 Hudson Street, New York, New York 10014, USA
Penguin Books Australia Ltd, Ringwood, Victoria, Australia
Penguin Books Canada Ltd, 10 Alcorn Avenue, Toronto, Ontario, Canada m4v 3b2
Penguin Books (NZ) Ltd, 182–190 Wairau Road, Auckland 10, New Zealand

Penguin Books Ltd, Registered Offices: Harmondsworth, Middlesex, England

First published by Viking 1992
Published in Puffin Books 1993
7 9 10 8 6

This selection copyright © Helen Cresswell, 1992
Illustrations copyright © Ainslie MacLeod, 1992
All rights reserved

The acknowledgements on pages 217–218 constitute an extension to this
copyright page

Printed in England by Clays Ltd, St Ives plc
Filmset in Bembo

Contents

Preface

Congratulations – whoever you are! You picked up this book (or even bought it) and want to read it. Ten out of ten. This means you have a high IQ. Well, higher than a duck's, at any rate, or an elephant's. Birds and animals don't laugh a lot, as you may have noticed. Ducks lay eggs, elephants never forget and human beings laugh.

The stories in this book are meant to be funny. They certainly made me laugh, and that is why I picked them. There are one or two things in here that I think should have a Government Warning: Do not read this while sitting alone on a bus or train or in any other public place. Sitting on your own, doubled up and snorting, with tears gushing from your eyes can be very embarrassing and makes other people nervous. I read *Three Men in a Boat* for the first time on a train journey. After a couple of chapters, I had practically cleared the carriage.

Several of the pieces are extracts from books, just to give you a taste. If they make you laugh – fine, you can go and get the book and have a really good wallow. If not, well, that simply means that you and I have a different sense of humour. But at least we *have* a sense of humour, and it always cheers me up no end to remember that this puts me one up on ducks, and elephants . . .

NB If not one single thing in here makes you laugh, then you are probably not a human being.

Helen Cresswell

William Leads a Better Life

RICHMAL CROMPTON

William needs no introduction. His adventures
have delighted children and adults alike for
over half a century. This story first appeared in
1926.

If you go far enough back it was Mr Strong, William's form master, who was responsible for the
whole thing. Mr Strong set, for homework, more
French than it was convenient for William to learn. It
happened that someone had presented William with
an electric motor, and the things one can do with an
electric motor are endless.

Who would waste the precious hours of a summer
evening over French verbs with an electric motor
simply crying out to be experimented on? Certainly
not William.

It wasn't as if there was any *sense* in French verbs.
They had been deliberately invented by someone with

a grudge against the race of boys – someone probably who'd slipped on a concealed slide or got in the way of a snowball or foolishly come within the danger zone of a catapult. Anyway, whoever it was had devised a mean form of revenge by inventing French verbs and, somehow or other, persuading schoolmasters to adopt them as one of their choicest tortures.

'Well, I never *will* wanter use 'em,' said William to his mother when she brought forward the time-honoured argument. 'I don't wanter talk to *any* French folks, an' if they wanter talk to me they can learn English. English's 's easy 's easy to talk. It's *silly* havin' other langwidges. I don' see why all the other countries shun't learn English 'stead of us learnin' other langwidges with no *sense* in 'em. English's *sense*.'

This speech convinced him yet more firmly of the foolishness of wasting his precious hours of leisure on such futile study, so he devoted all his time and energy to the electric motor. There was some *sense* in the electric motor. William spent a very happy evening.

In the morning, however, things somehow seemed different. He lay in bed and considered the matter. There was no doubt that Mr Strong could make himself extremely disagreeable over French verbs.

William remembered that he had threatened to make himself more disagreeable than usual if William did not know them 'next time'. This was 'next time' and William did not know them. William had not even attempted to learn them. The threats of Mr Strong had seemed feeble, purposeless, contemptible things last night when the electric motor threw its glamour over the whole world. This morning they didn't. They seemed suddenly much more real than the electric motor.

But surely it was possible to circumvent them. William was not the boy to give in weakly to any fate. He heard his mother's door opening, and, assuming an expression of intense suffering, called weakly, 'Mother.' Mrs Brown entered the room fully dressed.

'Aren't you up yet, William?' she said: 'Be quick or you'll be late for school.'

William intensified yet further his expression of suffering.

'I don' think I feel quite well enough to go to school this morning, mother, dear,' he said faintly.

Mrs Brown looked distressed. He had employed the ruse countless times before, but it never failed of its effect upon Mrs Brown. The only drawback was that Mr Brown, who was still about the house, was of a less trustful and compassionate nature.

Mrs Brown smoothed his pillow. 'Poor little boy,' she said tenderly, 'where is the pain?'

'All over,' said William, playing for safety.

'Dear! dear!' said Mrs Brown, much perturbed, as she left the room. 'I'll just go and fetch the thermometer.'

William disliked the thermometer. It was a soulless, unsympathetic thing. Sometimes, of course, a hot-water bottle, judiciously placed, would enlist its help, but that was not always easy to arrange.

To William's dismay his father entered the room with the thermometer.

'Well, William,' he said cheerfully, 'I hear you're too ill to go to school. That's a great pity, isn't it. I'm sure it's a grief to you?'

William turned up his eyes. 'Yes, father,' he said dutifully and suspiciously.

'Now where exactly is the pain and what sort of pain is it?'

William knew from experience that descriptions of non-existent pains are full of pitfalls. By a master-stroke he avoided them.

'It hurts me to talk,' he said.

'What sort of pain does it hurt you with?' said his father brutally.

William made some inarticulate noises, then closed his eyes with a moan of agony.

'I'll just step round and fetch the doctor,' said Mr Brown, still quite cheerful.

The doctor lived next door. William considered this a great mistake. He disliked the close proximity of doctors. They were equally annoying in real and imaginary diseases.

William made little brave reassuring noises to inform his father that he'd rather the doctor wasn't troubled and it was all right, and please no one was to bother about him, and he'd just stay in bed and probably be all right by the afternoon. But his father had already gone.

William lay in bed and considered his position.

Well, he was going to stick to it, anyway. He'd just make noises to the doctor, and they couldn't say he hadn't got a pain where he said he had if they didn't know where he said he had one. His mother came in and took his temperature. Fate was against him. There was no hot-water bottle handy. But he squeezed it as hard as he could in a vague hope that that would have some effect on it.

'It's normal, dear,' said his mother, relieved. 'I'm so glad.'

He made a sinister noise to imply that the malady was too deep-seated to be shown by an ordinary thermometer.

He could hear the doctor and his father coming up the stairs. They were laughing and talking. William, forgetting the imaginary nature of his complaint, felt a wave of indignation and self-pity.

The doctor came in breezily. 'Well, young man,' he said, 'what's the trouble?'

William made his noise. By much practice he was becoming an expert at the noise. It implied an intense desire to explain his symptoms, thwarted by physical incapability, and it thrilled with suffering bravely endured.

'Can't speak – is that it?' said the doctor.

'Yes, that's it,' said William, forgetting his role for the minute.

'Well – open your mouth, and let's have a look at your throat,' said the doctor.

William opened his mouth and revealed his throat.

The doctor inspected the recesses of that healthy and powerful organ.

'I see,' he said at last. 'Yes – very bad. But I can operate here and now, fortunately. I'm afraid I can't give an anaesthetic in this case, and I'm afraid it will be rather painful – but I'm sure he's a brave boy.'

William went pale and looked around desperately. French verbs were preferable to this.

'I'll wait just three minutes,' said the doctor kindly. 'Occasionally in cases like this the patient recovers his voice quite suddenly.' He took out his watch. William's father was watching the scene with an air of enjoyment that William found maddening. 'I'll give him just three minutes,' went on the doctor, 'and if the patient hasn't recovered the power of speech by then, I'll operate –'

The patient decided hastily to recover the power of speech.

'I can speak now,' he said with an air of surprise. 'Isn't it funny? I can talk quite ordinary now. It came on quite sudden.'

'No pain anywhere?' said the doctor.

'No,' said the patient quickly.

The patient's father stepped forward.

'Then you'd better get up as quickly as you can,' he said. 'You'll be late for school, but doubtless they'll know how to deal with that.'

They did know how to deal with that. They knew, too, how to deal with William's complete ignorance on the subject of French verbs. Excuses (and William

had many – some of them richly ingenious) were of
no avail. He went home to lunch embittered and
disillusioned with life.

'You'd think knowin' how to work a motor
engine'd be more *useful* than sayin' French verbs,' he
said. 'S'pose I turned out an engineer – well, wot
use'd French verbs be to me 'n I'd *have* to know how
to work a motor engine. An' I was so ill this mornin'
that the doctor wanted to do an operate on me, but I
said I *can't* miss school an' get all behind the others,
an' I came, awful ill, an' all they did was to carry on
something terrible 'cause I was jus' a minute or two
late an' jus' ha'n't had time to do those old French
verbs that aren't no *use* to anyone –'

Ginger, Henry and Douglas sympathized with him
for some time, then began to discuss the history
lesson. The history master, feeling for the moment as
bored with Edward the Sixth as were most of his
class, had given them a graphic account of the life of
St Francis of Assisi. He had spent the Easter holidays
at Assisi. William, who had been engaged in executing
creditable caricatures of Mr Strong and the doctor,
had paid little attention, but Ginger remembered it
all. It had been such a welcome change from William
the Conqueror. William began to follow the discus-
sion.

'Yes, but why'd he do it?' he said.

'Well, he jus' got kind of fed up with things an' he
had visions an' things an' he took some things of his
father's to sell to get money to start it –'

'*Crumbs!*' interpolated William. 'Wasn't his father mad?'

'Yes, but that din't matter. He was a saint, was Saint Francis, so he could sell his father's things if he liked, an' he 'n his frien's took the money an' got funny long sort of clothes an' went an' lived away in a little house by themselves, an' he uster preach to animals an' to people an' call everythin' "brother" an' "sister", and they cooked all their own stuff to eat an' –'

'Jolly fine it sounds,' said William enviously, 'an' did their people let 'em?'

'They couldn't' stop 'em,' said Ginger. 'An' Francis, he was the head one, an' the others all called themselves Franciscans, an' they built churches an' things.'

They had reached the gate of William's house now and William turned in slowly.

'G'bye till this afternoon,' called the others cheerfully.

Lunch increased still further William's grievances. No one inquired after his health, though he tried to look pale and ill, and refused a second helping of rice pudding with a meaning, 'No, thank you, not today. I would if I felt all right, thank you very much.' Even that elicited no anxious inquiries. No one, thought William, as he finished up the rice pudding in secret in the larder afterwards, no one else in the world, surely, had such a callous family. It would just serve them right to lose him altogether. It would just serve them right if he went off like St Francis and never came back.

He met Henry and Ginger and Douglas again as usual on the way to school.

'Beastly ole 'rithmetic,' said Henry despondently.

'Yes, an' then beastly ole jography,' sighed Douglas.

'Well,' said William, 'let's not go. I've been thinkin' a lot about that Saint man. I'd a lot sooner be a saint an' build things an' cook things an' preach to things than keep goin' to school an' learnin' the same ole things day after day an' day after day – all things like French verbs without any *sense* in them. I'd much sooner be a saint, wun't you?'

The other Outlaws looked doubtful, yet as though attracted by the idea.

'They wun't let us,' said Henry.

'They can't stop us bein' saints,' said William piously, 'an' doin' good an' preachin' – not if we have visions, an' I feel 's if I could have visions quite easy.'

The Outlaws had slackened their pace.

'What'd we have to do first?' said Ginger.

'Sell some of our fathers' things to get money,' said William firmly. ''S all right,' he went on, anticipating possible objections, 'he did, so I s'pose anyone can if they're settin' out to be saints – of course it would be different if we was jus' stealin', but bein' saints makes it diff'rent. Stands to reason saints can't steal.'

'Well, what'd we do *then*?' said Douglas.

'Then we find a place an' get the right sort of clothes to wear –'

'Seems sort of a waste of money,' said Henry

sternly, 'spendin' it on *clothes*. What sort of clothes were they?'

'He showed us a picture,' said Ginger, 'don' you remember? Sort of long things goin' right down to his feet.'

'Dressing-gowns'd do,' said Douglas excitedly.

'No, you're thinkin' of detectives,' said Henry firmly; 'detectives wear dressing-gowns.'

'No,' said William judicially. 'I don' see why dressing-gowns shun't do. Then we can save the money an' spend it on things to eat.'

'Where'll we live?'

'We oughter build a place, but till we've built it we can live in the old barn.'

'Where'll we get the animals to preach to?'

'Well, there's a farm just across the way from the barn, you know. We can start on Jumble an' then go on to the farm ones when we've had some practice.'

'An' what'll we be called? We can't be the Outlaws now we're saints, I s'pose?'

'What were they called?'

'Francisans . . . After Francis – he was the head one.'

'Well, if there's goin' to be any head one,' said William in a tone that precluded any argument on the subject, 'if there's going to be any head one, I'm going to be him.'

None of them denied to William the position of leader. It was his by right. He had always led, and he was a leader they were proud to follow.

'Well, they just put "cans" on to the end of his name,' said Henry. 'Franciscans. So we'll be William-cans –'

'Sounds kind of funny,' said Ginger dubiously.

'I think it sounds jolly fine,' said William proudly. 'I vote we start tomorrow, 'cause it's rather late to start today, an' anyway, it's Saturday tomorrow, so we can get well started for Monday, 'cause they're sure to make a fuss about our not turnin' up at school on Monday. You all come to the old barn d'rectly after breakfast tomorrow an' bring your dressing-gowns an' somethin' of your father's to sell –'

The first meeting of the Williamcans was held directly after breakfast the next morning. They had all left notes dictated by William on their bedroom mantelpieces announcing that they were now saints and had left home for ever.

They deposited their dressing-gowns on the floor of the old barn and then inspected the possessions that they had looted from their unsuspecting fathers. William had appropriated a pair of slippers, not because he thought their absence would be undetected (far from it) or because he thought they would realize vast wealth (again far from it), but it happened that they were kept in the fender-box of the morning-room, and William had found himself alone there for a few minutes that morning, and slippers can be concealed quite easily beneath one's coat. He could have more easily appropriated something of his mother's, but William liked to do things properly. Saint Francis had sold something of his father's, so Saint William would do the same. Douglas took from his pocket an ink-stand, purloined from his father's desk; Ginger had two ties and Henry a pair of gloves.

They looked at their spoils with proud satisfaction.

'We oughter get a good deal of money for *these*,' said William. 'How much did *he* get, d'you know?'

'No, he never said,' said Ginger.

'We'd better not put on our saint robes yet – not till we've been down to the village to sell the things. Then we'll put 'em on an' start preachin' an' things.'

'Din' we oughter wear round-hoop-sort-of-things on our heads?' said Henry. 'They do in pictures. What d'you call 'em? – Haloes.'

'You don' get *them* till you're dead,' said Ginger with an air of wisdom.

'Well, I don't see what good they are to anyone *dead*,' said Henry, rather aggrieved.

'No, we've gotter do things *right*,' said William sternly. 'If the real saints waited till they was dead, we will, too. Anyway, let's go an' sell the things first. An' remember call everything else "brother" or "sister".'

'*Everything?*'

'Yes – he did – the other man did.'

'You've gotter call me *Saint* William now, Ginger.'

'All right, you call me Saint Ginger.'

'All right, I'm goin' to – Saint Ginger –'

'Saint William.'

'All right.'

'Well, where you goin' to sell the slippers?'

'*Brother* slippers,' corrected William. 'Well, I'm goin' to sell brother slippers at Mr Marsh's 'f he'll buy 'em.'

'An' I'll take brother ties along, too,' said Ginger. 'An' Henry take brother gloves, an' Douglas brother inkstand.'

'*Sister* inkstand,' said Douglas. 'William –'

'Saint William,' corrected William, patiently.

'Well, Saint William said we could call things brother *or* sister, an' my inkstand's goin' to be sister.'

'*Swank!*' said St Ginger severely, 'always wanting to be diff'rent from other people!'

Mr Marsh kept a second-hand shop at the end of the village. In his window reposed side by side a motley collection of battered and despised household goods.

He had a less optimistic opinion of the value of brothers slippers and ties and gloves and sister inkstand than the saints.

He refused to allow them more than sixpence each.

'*Mean!*' exploded St William indignantly as soon as they had emerged from Mr Marsh's dingy little sanctum to the village street and the light of day. 'I call him sim'ly *mean*. That's what *I* call him.'

'I s'pose now we're saints,' said St Ginger piously, 'that we've gotter forgive folks what wrong us like that.'

'I'm not goin' to be *that* sort of a saint,' said St William firmly.

Back at the barn they donned their dressing-gowns, St Henry still grumbling at not being able to wear the 'little hoop' on his head.

'Now what d'we do *first*?' said St Ginger energetically, as he fastened the belt of his dressing-gown.

'Well, anyway, why can't we cut little bits of our hair at the top like they have in pictures?' said St Henry disconsolately, 'that'd be better than *nothin'*.'

This idea rather appealed to the saints. St Douglas discovered a penknife and began to operate at once on St Henry, but the latter saint's yells of agony soon brought the proceedings to a premature end.

'Well, *you* s'gested it,' said St Douglas, rather hurt, 'an' I was doin' it as gently as I could.'

'*Gently!*' groaned Henry, still nursing his saintly head. 'You were tearing it out by the roots.'

'Well, come *on!*' said St Ginger impatiently, 'let's begin now. What did you say we were goin' to do first?'

'Preachin' to animals is the first thing,' said William in his most business-like manner. 'I've got Brother Jumble here. Ginger – I mean St Ginger, you hold Brother Jumble while I preach to him 'cause he's not used to it, an' he might try to run away, an' St Henry an' St Douglas go out an' preach to birds. The St Francis man did a lot of preachin' to birds. They came an' sat on his arms. See if you can gettem to do that. Well now, let's start. Ginger – I mean St Ginger – you catch hold of Brother Jumble.'

Henry and Douglas departed. Douglas's dressing-gown, made by a thrifty mother with a view to Douglas's further growth, was slightly too big and tripped him over every few steps. Henry's was made of bath towelling and was rather conspicuous in design. They made their way slowly across a field and into a neighbouring wood.

St Ginger encircled the reluctant Jumble with his arms, and St William stood up to preach.

'Dearly beloved Jumble –' he began.

'Brother Jumble,' corrected St Ginger, with triumph. He liked to catch the founder of the order tripping.

Jumble, under the delusion that something was expected of him, sat up and begged.

'Dearly beloved Brother Jumble,' repeated William. He stopped and cleared his throat in the manner of all speakers who are not sure what to say next.

Jumble, impatient of the other saint's encircling arms, tried another trick, that of standing on his head. Standing on his head was the title given to the performance by Jumble's owner. In reality it consisted of rubbing the top of his head on the ground. None of his legs left the ground, but William always called it 'Jumble standing on his head', and was inordinately proud of it.

'Look at him,' he said, 'isn't that jolly clever? An' no one told him to. Jus' did it without anyone tellin' him to. I bet there's not many dogs like him. I bet he's the cleverest dog there is in England. I wun't mind sayin' he's the cleverest dog there is in the world. I wun't –'

'I thought you was preachin' to him, not talkin' about him,' said St Ginger, sternly. Ginger, who was not allowed to possess a dog, tired occasionally of hearing William sing the praises of his.

'Oh, yes,' said St William with less enthusiasm. 'I'll start all over again. Dearly beloved Brother Jumble – I say, what did that St Francis *say* to the animals?'

'Dunno,' said St Ginger vaguely, 'I s'pect he jus' told 'em to – well, to do good an' that sort of thing.'

'Dearly beloved Brother Jumble,' said William again, 'you mus' – do good an' – an' stop chasin' cats. Why,' he said proudly, 'there's not a cat in this village that doesn't run when it sees Jumble comin'. I bet he's the best dog for chasin' cats anywhere round *this* part of England. I bet –'

Jumble, seizing his moment for escape, tore himself from St Ginger's unwary arms, and leapt up ecstatically at William.

'Good old Jumble,' said the saint affectionately. 'Good old boy!'

At this point the other two saints returned.

'Well, did you find any birds?' said St William.

'There was heaps of birds,' said St Douglas in an exasperated tone of voice, 'but the minute I started preachin' they all flew off. They din' seem to know how to *act* with saints. They din' seem to know they'd got to sit on our arms an' things. Made us feel *mad* – anyway, we gotter thrush's egg and Henry – I mean St Henry – jus' wanted one of those –'

'Well,' said St William rather sternly, 'I don' think

it's the right thing for saints to do – to go preachin' to birds an' then takin' their eggs – I mean their brother eggs.'

'There was *lots* more,' said Henry. 'They *like* you jus' takin' one. It makes it less trouble for 'em hatchin' 'em out.'

'Well, anyway,' said William, 'let's get on with this animal business. P'raps the tame ones'll be better. Let's go across to Jenks' farm an' try on them.'

They crept rather cautiously into the farmyard. The feud between Farmer Jenks and the Outlaws was one of long standing. He would probably not realize that the Williamcans were a saintly organization whose every action was inspired by a love of mankind. He would probably imagine that they were still the old unregenerate Outlaws.

'I'll do brother cows,' said St William, 'an' St Ginger do brother pigs, and St Douglas do brother goats, an' St Henry do sister hens.'

They approached their various audiences. Ginger leant over the pigsty. Then he turned to William, who was already striking an attitude before his congregation of cows, and said: 'I say, what've I gotter *say* to 'em?'

At that moment brother goat, being approached too nearly by St Douglas, butted the saintly stomach and St Douglas sat down suddenly and heavily. Brother goat, evidently enjoying this form of entertainment, returned to the charge. St Douglas fled to the accompaniment of an uproarious farmyard commotion.

Farmer Jenks appeared, and, seeing his old enemies,

the Outlaws, actually within his precincts, he uttered a yell of fury and darted down upon them. The saints fled swiftly, St Douglas holding up his too-flowing robe as he went. Brother goat had given St Douglas a good start and he reached the farm first.

'Well,' said St William, panting, 'I've *finished* with preachin' to animals. They must have changed a good bit since *his* time. That's all *I* can say.'

'Well, what'll we do *now*?' said St Ginger.

'I should almost think it's time for dinner,' said William. 'Must be after two, I should think.'

No one knew the time. Henry possessed a watch which had been given to him by a great-uncle. Though it may possibly have had some value as an antique, it had not gone for over twenty years. Henry, however, always wore it, and generally remembered to move its hands to a correct position whenever he passed a clock. This took a great deal of time and trouble, but Henry was proud of his watch and liked it to be as nearly right as possible. He consulted it now. He had put it right by his family's hall clock as he came out after breakfast, so its fingers stood at half-past nine. He returned it to his pocket hastily before the others could see the position of the fingers.

'Yes,' he said, with the air of an oracle, 'it's about dinner-time.' Though they all knew that Henry's watch had never gone, yet it had a certain prestige.

'Well, we've gotter *buy* our dinner,' said William. 'S'pose two of us goes down to the village, an' buys it now with the two shillings we got for sellin' our fathers' things. We've gotter buy all our meals now like what *they* did.'

'Well, how d'we get the money when we've finished this? We can't go *on* sellin' our fathers' things. They'd get so mad.'

'We beg from folks after that,' said Ginger, who was the only one who had paid much attention to the story of the life of St Francis.

'Well, I bet they won't give us much if *I* know 'em,' said William bitterly. 'I bet both folks *an'* animals must've been nicer in those times.'

It was decided that Douglas and Henry should go down to the village to purchase provisions for the meal. It was decided also that they should go in their dressing-gowns.

'*They* always did,' said Ginger firmly, 'and folks may's well get used to us goin' about like that.'

'Oh, yes!' said Douglas bitterly. ''S easy to talk like that when you're not goin' down to the shop.'

Mr Moss, the proprietor of the village sweet-shop, held his sides with laughter when he saw them.

'Well, I never!' he said. 'Well, I never! What boys you are for a joke, to be sure!'

'It's not a joke,' said Henry. 'We're Williamcans.'

Douglas had caught sight of the clock on the desk behind the counter.

'I say!' he said. 'It's only eleven o'clock.'

Henry took out his watch.

'Oh, yes,' he said, as if he had made a mistake when he looked at it before.

For their midday meal the two saints purchased a large bag of chocolate creams, another of bull's-eyes, and, to form the more solid part of the meal, four cream buns.

Ginger and William and Jumble were sitting comfortably in the old barn when the two emissaries returned.

'*We've* had a nice time!' exploded St Henry. 'All the boys in the place runnin' after us an' shoutin' at us.'

'You should've just stood still an' *preached* to 'em,' said the founder of the order calmly.

'*Preached* to 'em!' repeated Henry. 'They wun't have listened. They was shoutin' an' throwin' things an' running at us.'

'What'd you do?'

'Run,' said the gallant saint simply. 'An' Douglas has tore his robe, an' I've fallen in the mud in mine.'

'Well, they've gotter last you all the rest of your life,' said St William, 'so you oughter take more care of 'em,' and added with more interest, 'what've you got for dinner?'

They displayed their purchases and their choice was warmly and unanimously approved by the saints.

'Wish we'd thought of something to drink,' said Henry.

But William, with a smile of pride, brought out from his pocket a bottle of dark liquid.

'I *thought* of that,' he said, holding it out with a flourish, 'have a drink of brother lik'rice water.'

Not to be outdone, Douglas took up one of the bags.

'An' have a sister cream bun,' he said loudly.

When they had eaten and drunk to repletion they rested for a short time from their labours. William had meant to fill in time by preaching to Jumble, but decided instead to put Jumble through his tricks.

'I s'pose they *know* now at home that we've gone for good,' said Henry with a sigh.

Ginger looked out of the little windows anxiously.

'Yes. I only hope to goodness they won't come an' try to fetch us back,' he said.

But he need not have troubled. Each family thought that the missing member was having lunch with one of the others, and felt no anxiety, only a great relief. And none of the notes upon the mantelpieces had been found.

'What'll we do *now*?' said William, rousing himself at last.

'*They* built a church,' said Ginger.

'Crumbs!' said William, taken aback. 'Well, we can't do that, can we?'

'Oh, I dunno,' said Ginger vaguely, 'jus' keep on putting stones on each other. It was quite a little church.'

'Well, it'd take us more'n quite a little time.'

'Yes, but we've gotter do *something* 'stead of goin' to school, an' we may's well do that.'

''S almost as bad as goin' to school,' said William gloomily. 'An' where'd they get the stones?'

'They jus' found 'em lying about.'

'Well, come on,' said William, rising with a re-
signed air and gathering the folds of his dressing-gown
about him, 'let's see 'f we can find any lyin' about.'

They wandered down the road. They still wore
their dressing-gowns, but they wore them with a sheep-
ish air and went cautiously and furtively. Already
their affection for their saintly garb was waning. Fortunately, the road was deserted. They looked up and
down, then St Ginger gave a yell of triumph and
pointed up the road. The road was being mended,
and there lay by the roadside, among other materials,
a little heap of wooden bricks. Moreover, the bricks
were unguarded and unattended.

It was the British workman's dinner hour, and the
British workman was spending it in the nearest pub.

'Crumbs!' said the Williamcans in delight.

They fell upon the wooden bricks and bore them
off in triumph. Soon they had a pile of them just
outside the barn where they had resolved to build the
church – almost enough, the head of the order decided,
to begin on. But as they paid their last visit for bricks
they met a little crowd of other children, who burst
into loud jeering cries.

'Look at 'em ... Dear little girlies ... wearin' nice
long pinnies ... Oh, my! Oh *don'* they look sweet?
Hello, little darlins!'

William flung aside his saintly robe and closed with
the leader. The other saints closed with the others.
Quite an interesting fight ensued. The saints, smaller

in number and size than the other side, most decidedly got the best of it, though not without many casualties. The other side took to its heels.

St William, without much enthusiasm, picked his saintly robe up from the mud and began to put it on.

'Don' see much *sense* in wearin' these things,' he said.

'You ought to have *preached* to 'em, not fought 'em,' said Ginger severely.

'Well, I bet *he* wun't've preached to 'em if they'd started makin' fun of him. He'd've fought 'em all right.'

'No, he wun't,' said Ginger firmly, 'he din't b'lieve in fightin'.'

William's respect for his prototype, already on the wane, waned still further. But he did not lightly relinquish anything he had once undertaken.

'Well, anyway,' he said, 'let's get a move on buildin' that church.'

They returned to the field and their little pile of bricks.

But the British workman had also returned from his dinner hour at the nearest pub, and had discovered the disappearance of the larger part of his material. With lurid oaths he had tracked them down and came upon the saints just as they had laboriously laid the first row of bricks for the first wall. He burst upon them with fury.

They did not stay to argue. They fled. Henry cast aside his splendid robe of multi-coloured bath towelling into a ditch to accelerate his flight. The British workman tired first. He went back after throwing a brick at their retreating forms and informing them lustily that he knew their fathers an' he'd go an' tell them, danged if he wouldn't, and they'd find themselves in jail – saucy little 'ounds – danged if they wouldn't.

The Williamcans waited till all was clear before they emerged from their hiding-places and gathered together dejectedly in the barn. William and Ginger had sustained black eyes and bleeding noses as the result of the fight with the village children. Douglas had fallen during the flight from the British workman and caught Henry on his ankle, and he limped painfully. Their faces had acquired an extraordinary amount of dirt.

They sat down and surveyed each other.

'Seems to me,' said William, 'it's a *wearin'* kind of life.'

It was cold. It had begun to rain.

'Brother rain,' remarked Ginger brightly.

'Yes, an' I should think it's about sister tea-time,' said William dejectedly; 'an' what we goin' to buy it – her – with? How're we goin' to get money?'

'I've got sixpence at home,' said Henry. 'I mean I've gotter brother sixpence at home.'

But William had lost his usual optimism.

'Well, that won't keep all of us for the rest of our lives, will it?' he said; 'an' I don't feel like startin' beggin' after the time I've had today. I haven't got much *trust* in folks.'

'Henry – I mean, St Henry – oughter give his brother sixpence to the poor,' said Ginger piously. '*They* uster give all their money to the poor.'

'*Give* it?' said William incredulously. 'An' get nothin' back for it?'

'No – jus' give it,' said Ginger.

William thought deeply for a minute.

'Well,' he said at last, voicing the opinion of the whole order, 'I'm jus' about sick of bein' a saint. I'd sooner be a pirate or a Red Indian any day.'

The rest looked relieved.

'Yes, I've had *enough*,' said William, 'and let's stop callin' each other saints an' brothers an' sisters an' wearin' dressing-gowns. There's no *sense* in it. An' I'm almost dyin' of cold an' hunger an' I'm goin' home.'

They set off homeward through the rain, cold and wet and bruised and very hungry. The saintly repast of cream buns and chocolate creams and bull's-eyes, though enjoyable at the time, had proved singularly un-sustaining.

But their troubles were not over.

As they went through the village they stopped in front of Mr Marsh's shop window. There in the very middle were William's father's slippers, Douglas' father's inkstand, Ginger's father's tie and Henry's father's gloves – all marked at 1/-. The hearts of the Williamcans stood still. Their fathers would probably not yet have returned from Town. The thought of their seeing their prized possessions reposing in Mr

Marsh's window marked 1/- was a horrid one. It had not seemed to matter this morning. This morning they were leaving their homes for ever. It did seem to matter this evening. This evening they were returning to their homes.

They entered the shop and demanded them. Mr Marsh was adamant. In the end Henry fetched his sixpence, William a treasured penknife, Ginger a compass, and Douglas a broken steam engine, and their paternal possessions were handed back.

They went home dejectedly through the rain. The British workman might or might not fulfil his threat of calling on their parents. The saintly career which had looked so roseate in the distance had turned out, as William aptly described it, 'wearin''. Life was full of disillusions.

William discovered with relief that his father had not yet come home. He returned the slippers, somewhat damp, to the fender-box. He put his muddy dressing-gown beneath the bed. He found his note unopened and unread, still upon the mantelpiece. He tore it up. He tidied himself superficially. He went downstairs.

'Had a nice day, dear?' said his mother.

He disdained to answer the question.

'There's just an hour before tea,' she went on; 'hadn't you better be doing your homework, dear?'

He considered. One might as well drink of tragedy the very dregs while one was about it. It would be a rotten ending to a rotten day. Besides, there was no doubt about it – Mr Strong was going to make himself very disagreeable indeed, if he didn't know those French verbs for Monday. He might as well – if he'd had any idea how rotten it was being a saint he jolly well wouldn't have wasted a whole Saturday over it. He took down a French grammar and sat down moodily before it without troubling to put it right way up.

You Don't Look Very Poorly

Adapted from *Crummy Mummy and Me*

ANNE FINE

This was the first of what turned out to be several stories about Minna and her unusual family.

You don't exactly *ask* to get sick, do you? I mean, you don't go round *inviting* germs and viruses to move in and do their worst to your body. You don't actually *apply* for trembling legs and feeling shivery, and a head that's had a miniature steel band practising for a carnival in it all night.

And if you should happen to mention to your own mother that you feel absolutely terrible, you would expect a bit of sympathy, wouldn't you?

I wouldn't. Not any more.

'You don't *look* very poorly.'

That's what she said. And she said it suspiciously,

too, as if I was one of those people who's always making excuses to stay off school and spend the day wrapped in a downie on the sofa watching *Bagpuss* and *Playschool* and *Pebble Mill at One*.

'Well, I feel absolutely rotten.'

'You don't look it.'

'I'm sorry!' I snapped. (I was getting pretty cross.) 'Sorry I can't manage a bright-green face for you! Or purple spots on my belly! Or all my hair falling out! But I feel rotten just the same!'

And I burst into tears.

(Now that's not like me.)

'Now that's not like you,' said Mum, sounding sympathetic at last. 'You must be a little bit off today.'

'I am not *off*,' I snarled through my tears. 'I'm not leftover milk. Or rotten fish.'

'There, there,' Mum soothed. 'Don't fret, Minna. Don't get upset. You just hop straight back up those stairs like a good poppet, and in a minute I'll bring something nice up on a tray, and you can have a quiet day in bed, with Mum looking after you until you feel better.'

That was a bit more like it, as I think you'll agree. So I stopped snivelling and went back to bed. I didn't exactly hop straight back up those stairs because I was feeling so crummy and weak I could barely drag myself up hanging on to the banisters; but I got up somehow, and put on my dressing-gown and buttoned it right up to the top to keep my chest warm, and plumped up my pillows so I could sit comfortably, and switched on my little plastic frog reading-lamp, and folded my hands in my lap, and I waited.

And I waited.

And I waited.

(In case you're wondering, I was waiting for Mum to bring me up something nice on a tray and look after me until I felt better.)

She never came.

Oh, I'm sure that she *meant* to come. I'm sure she had every intention of coming. I'm sure it wasn't her fault the milkman came and needed paying, and it took time to work out what she owed because he'd been away for two weeks on his holiday in Torremolinos.

And I'm sure it wasn't Mum's fault that he took the opportunity to park his crate of bottles down on the doorstep and tell her all about the way some sneaky people always bagged the best pool-loungers by creeping down at dead of night and dropping their swimming towels over them; and how his wife's knees burned and peeled but none of the rest of her, even though all of her was out in the sun for the same amount of time; and how his daughter Meryl came home to her job at the Halifax with a broken heart because of some fellow called Miguel Angel Gippini Lopez de Rego, who danced like a fury but turned out to be engaged to a Spanish girl working in Barcelona.

Oh, it wasn't Mum's fault that she had to listen to

all that before she could get away to bring me up something nice on a tray and look after me until I was better. But I could hear them talking clearly enough on the doorstep. And I don't actually recall hearing her say firmly but politely: 'Excuse me, Mr Hooper, but Minna's in bed feeling terrible, and I must get back upstairs, so I'll listen to all the rest tomorrow.' I heard quite a bit; but I didn't hear that.

As soon as the milkman had chinked off next door, I thought I heard Mum making for the bottom of the stairs. But she never got there.

'Yeeeoooooowwwwwwwaaaaa*AAAAAAAAAAAE-EEEEEWWW*!'

You guessed it. My baby sister woke up.

And I suppose it wasn't Mum's fault that Miranda needed her nappy changing. And that there weren't any dry ones because we don't have a tumble-drier and it had been raining for three solid days. And Mum had forgotten to pick up another packet of disposables last time she practically *swam* down to the shops.

So Mum decided the simplest thing would be to park Miranda in the playpen where little accidents don't matter. It wasn't her fault it took for ever to drag it out of the cupboard because she had dumped my sledge, and the dress-up box, and all the empty jars she's saving for Gran right in front of it. Or that she had to fetch the damp nappies off the line and drape them over the rack in the kitchen.

And I suppose it's understandable that while she

was shaking out the damp nappies, she should glance out of the window at the grey skies and think about nipping down to the launderette with the rest of the washing and handing it to Mrs Hajee to do in the machines, since it really didn't look as if it would ever stop raining.

So I suppose it does make sense that the very next thing I heard on my quiet day in bed was Mum bellowing up the stairs:

'Minna! *Minna!* Look after the baby for a few minutes, will you, while I nip down to the launderette? She's perfectly happy in her playpen with her toys. Just come down if she starts to squawk.'

Fine. Lovely. Sure. Here am I, feeling really terrible and looking forward to something nice on a tray and being looked after until I feel better, and suddenly I'm looking after the baby! Fine. Lovely. Sure.

To be quite fair to Mum, she didn't stay out any longer than was absolutely necessary. There was the launderette, of course. And then she had to get the disposable nappies or Miranda would have had to spend the whole morning sitting on her cold bottom in the playpen, waiting for the ones in the kitchen to dry. And while she was in the supermarket she did pick up bread, and a quarter of sliced ham, and a few oranges and a couple of other things, making too many to get through the quick check-out. And there were really long queues at all the others because it was pension-day morning. And she did just pop into the newsagent's on her way home as well. And, yes, she did stop on the corner for a second, but that was just to be polite to the Lollipop Lady who told her that, whatever it was I'd got, there was a lot of it about, and Mum ought to be really careful or she'd come down with it as well.

And then she came straight home. She *says* she was out for no more than five minutes at the very most. But I've a watch, so I know better.

Then, at last, she came up to my room. She had Miranda tucked under one arm, all bare bottom and wriggles, and she was carrying a tray really high in the air, practically above her head, so my sister couldn't upset it with all her flailing arms and legs. It was so high I couldn't see what was on it from the bed.

'I don't know how these nurses do it,' said Mum. 'They should have medals pinned on their chests, not watches.'

I looked at mine. It was exactly half past ten. (I fell sick at 8.23.)

'If you were a nurse,' I said, 'you would have got the sack two hours ago.'

'I'd like to see you do any better,' she snapped back, sharpish.

'I bet I would,' I told her. 'I bet if *you* were sick, it wouldn't take *me* two whole hours to bring you something nice on a tray.'

'I should wait till you see what there is on the tray before you start grumbling,' Mum warned. And then she lowered it on to the bed in front of me.

And there was a cup of very milky coffee with bubbles on top in my favourite fat china bear mug, and a huge orange cut into the thinnest possible circular slices, just how I like it when I want to nibble at the peel as well. And a chocolate-biscuit bar and the latest *Beano* and *Dandy*, and a pack of twenty brand-new fine-tipped felt pens.

I felt dead guilty for being so grumpy.

'I'm sorry I said you'd get the sack as a nurse.'

'Oh, that's all right,' Mum answered cheerfully. She flipped Miranda over and put a nappy on her before there was trouble and even more laundry. 'It's a well-known fact that it's even harder to be a good patient than a good nurse.'

'Is that true?'

'Certainly.'

And then, with my baby sister safe at last, Mum sat down on my bed and took a break.

I thought about what she said quite a lot while I was getting better. As I sipped my coffee, and nibbled my orange circles, and read my *Beano*, and made my chocolate biscuit last as long as I could while I was drawing with my brand-new felt pens, I wondered what sort of patient Mum would make. She isn't famous in this house for long-suffering meekness or sunny patience.

And I wondered what sort of nurse I'd make – sensitive, deft, unflappable, efficient . . .

I'd no idea I would find out so soon.

It was only two days later, on Saturday morning, that Mum leaned over the banisters and called down:

'Minna, I feel just awful. Awful.'

'You don't *look* very poorly.'

(I didn't mean it that way. It just popped out.)

You'd have thought I was trying to suggest she was faking.

'I may not *look* it, but I *am*,' she snapped. 'I feel as if I've been left out all night in the rain, and my bones have gone soggy, and hundreds of spiteful little men with steel boots are holding a stamping competition in my brain.'

Personally, even without the Lollipop Lady saying there was a lot of it about, I would have recognized the symptoms at once.

I was determined to show Mum what proper nursing ought to be.

'You go straight back to bed,' I ordered. 'I'll take care of you, and everything else. You tuck yourself in comfortably, and I'll bring up something nice on a tray.'

Mum swayed a little against the banisters. She did look pale.

'You are an angel, Minna,' she said faintly. And wrapping her shiny black skull-and-crossbones dressing-gown more closely around her string-vest nightie, she staggered back into the bedroom.

I don't have to tell you about my plan, do I? You'll already have guessed. Yes, I was going to rush back into the kitchen and spread a tray with lovely, tempting treats for an invalid's breakfast – treats like a cup of tea made just the way Mum really likes it, golden-pale, not that lovely, thick, murky, dark sludge favoured by me and Gran. (We joke that Mum's tea is too weak to crawl out of the pot.) And I was going to pick a tiny posy of flowers from the garden, and arrange them in one of the pretty china egg cups.

And I was going to bring the tray up without delay.

Guess what went wrong first. No, don't bother. I'll tell you. First, I locked myself out. Honestly. Me, Minna. The only one in the house who *never* does it. I did it. I was so keen to get my tray arranged that I stepped out of the back door into the garden to find the flowers without checking the latch.

Clunk!

The moment I heard the door close behind me, I realized. I could have kicked myself in the shins. I picked my way around to the front, just on the off-chance that the front door was unlocked. But I knew it wouldn't be, and of course it wasn't.

I stood there, thinking. I had two choices. I could ring the doorbell and drag poor, shaking, deathly pale Mum from her bed of sickness and down the stairs to let me in; or I could slip next door to old Mrs Pitopoulos, ring her bell instead, and ask to borrow the spare key to our house she keeps for emergencies in an old cocoa tin under her sink.

I knew which a good nurse would do. I went next door and rang the bell.

No answer.

I rang again.

Still no answer.

Suddenly I noticed a faint scrabbling overhead. I looked up, and there was Mrs Pitopoulos in her quilted dressing-gown, fighting the stiff window-catch with her arthritic fingers.

She couldn't budge it, so she just beckoned me inside the house.

I tried the front door. It was locked. I went round the back, and that door opened. I picked my way through the furry sea of all her pet cats rubbing their arched backs against my legs, so pleased to see me, and went upstairs.

Mrs Pitopoulos was sitting on the edge of her bed. Her face looked like a wrinkled sack, and her wig was all crooked.

'You look very poorly,' I told her.

I couldn't help it. It just popped out.

'Oh, Minna,' she said. 'I feel terrible, terrible. My legs are rubber, and there are red-hot nails in my head.'

'I've had that,' I said. 'Mum's got it now. The Lollipop Lady says that there's lots of it about.'

When she heard this, Mrs Pitopoulos began to look distinctly better. Maybe when you're that age and you get sick, you think whatever it is has come to get you. At any rate, she tugged her wig round on her head, and even the wrinkles seemed to flatten out a bit.

'Minna,' she said. 'Would you do me a great favour, and feed my hungry cats?'

'What about you?' I said. 'Have you had anything this morning?'

'Oh, I'm not hungry,' Mrs Pitopoulos declared. But then she cocked her head on one side, and wondered about it. And then she added:

'Maybe I do feel just a little bit peckish. Yesterday my sister brought me all these lovely things: new-laid brown speckled eggs and home-made bread and a tiny pot of fresh strawberry jam. But what I'd really like is . . .' (Her eyes were gleaming, and she looked miles better.) 'What I'd really like is a bowl of Heinz tomato soup with bits of white bread floating on the top.'

Even I can cook that.

And so I did. And fed her cats. And she was so pleased when I brought the soup up to her on a tray that she pressed on me all the little gifts her sister had brought round the day before: the new-laid brown speckled eggs and home-made bread and tiny pot of fresh strawberry jam – oh, and the door key of course.

Mum was astonished when I brought the tray up. I thought she must have been asleep. She looked as if she had been dozing. She heaved herself upright against the pillows, and I laid the tray down on her knees.

'Minna!' she cried. 'Oh, how lovely! Look at the flowers!'

'Wait till you've tasted the food,' I said.

I could tell that she didn't really feel much like eating. But she was determined not to hurt my feelings, so she reached out and took one of the strips of hot buttered toast made from the home-made bread.

She nibbled the crust politely.

'Delicious,' she said. And then, 'Mmm. *Delicious*.'

She couldn't help dipping the next strip of toast into the new-laid brown speckled soft-boiled egg.

'Mmmm!' she cried. 'This is *wonderful*.'

After the egg was eaten, she still had two strips of toast left. She spread one with the fresh strawberry jam, and off she went again.

'Mmmm! *Marvellous!*'

She went into raptures over the golden-pale tea. (I reckoned I'd have a battle ever forcing her back to medium-brown, when she felt well again.) And then she leaned back against the pillows, smiling.

She looked a lot better.

'I'll bring you some more, if you'd like it,' I offered.

'You are the *very best nurse*,' Mum declared. 'You managed all this, and so quickly too!'

Now I was sure she'd been dozing. I'd taken *ages*.

'You're the *very best patient*,' I returned the compliment. 'You don't notice what's going on, or how long it takes!'

'Silly,' she said, and snuggled back under the bedcovers.

I think she must have thought I was joking.

The Young Visiters

DAISY ASHFORD

This book was written in pencil in a notebook by nine-year-old Daisy Ashford at the end of the last century. It is a child's-eye view of grown-ups and it is not meant to be funny – which is probably why it is. Here are the first two chapters.

QUITE A YOUNG GIRL

Mr Salteena was an elderly man of 42 and was fond of asking peaple to stay with him. He had quite a young girl staying with him of 17 named Ethel Monticue. Mr Salteena had dark short hair and mustache and wiskers which were very black and twisty. He was middle sized and he had very pale blue eyes. He had a pale brown suit but on Sundays he had

a black one and he had a topper every day as he thorght it more becoming. Ethel Monticue had fair hair done on the top and blue eyes. She had a blue velvit frock which had grown rather short in the sleeves. She had a black straw hat and kid gloves.

One morning Mr Salteena came down to brekfast and found Ethel had come down first which was strange. Is the tea made Ethel he said rubbing his hands. Yes said Ethel and such a quear shaped parcel has come for you. Yes indeed it was a quear shape parcel it was a hat box tied down very tight and a letter stuffed between the string. Well well said Mr Salteena parcels do turn quear I will read the letter first and so saying he tore open the letter and this is what it said

My dear Alfred

I want you to come for a stop with me so I have sent you a top hat wraped up in tishu paper inside the box. Will you wear it staying with me because it is very uncommon. Please bring one of your young ladies whichever is the prettiest in the face.

I remain Yours truely
Bernard Clark.

Well said Mr Salteena I shall take you to stay Ethel and fancy him sending me a top hat. Then Mr S. opened the box and there lay the most splendid top hat of a lovly rich tone rarther like grapes with a ribbon round compleat.

Well said Mr Salteena peevishly I dont know if I shall like it the bow of the ribbon is too flighty for my age. Then he sat down and eat the egg which

Ethel had so kindly laid for him. After he had finished his meal he got down and began to write to Bernard Clark he ran up stairs on his fat legs and took out his blotter with a loud sniff and this is what he wrote

MY DEAR BERNARD

Certinly I shall come and stay with you next Monday I will bring Ethel Monticue commonly called Miss M. She is very active and pretty. I do hope I shall enjoy myself with you. I am fond of digging in the garden and I am parshial to ladies if they are nice I suppose it is my nature. I am not quite a gentleman but you would hardly notice it but cant be helped anyhow. We will come by the 3-15.

Your old and valud friend

ALFRED SALTEENA.

Perhaps my readers will be wondering why Bernard Clark had asked Mr Salteena to stay with him. He was a lonely man in a remote spot and he liked peaple and partys but he did not know many. What rot muttered Bernard Clark as he read Mr Salteenas letter. He was rarther a presumshious man.

STARTING GAILY

When the great morning came Mr Salteena did not have an egg for his brekfast in case he should be sick on the jorney.

What top hat will you wear asked Ethel.

I shall wear my best black and white alpacka coat to keep off the dust and flies replied Mr Salteena.

I shall put some red ruge on my face said Ethel because I am very pale owing to the drains in this house.

You will look very silly said Mr Salteena with a dry laugh.

Well so will you said Ethel in a snappy tone and she ran out of the room with a very superier run throwing out her legs behind and her arms swinging in rithum.

Well said the owner of the house she has a most idiotick run.

Presently Ethel came back in her best hat and a lovly velvit coat of royal blue. Do I look nice in my get up she asked.

Mr Salteena survayed her. You look rarther rash my dear your colors dont quite match your face but never mind I am just going up to say goodbye to Rosalind the housemaid.

Well dont be long said Ethel. Mr S. skipped upstairs to Rosalinds room. Goodbye Rosalind he said I shall be back soon and I hope I shall enjoy myself.

I make no doubt of that sir said Rosalind with a blush as Mr Salteena silently put 2/6 on the dirty toilet cover.

Take care of your bronkitis said Mr S. rarther bashfully and he hastilly left the room waving his hand carelessly to the housemaid.

Come along cried Ethel powdering her nose in the

hall let us get into the cab. Mr Salteena did not care
for powder but he was an unselfish man so he dashed
into the cab. Sit down said Ethel as the cabman waved
his whip you are standing on my luggage. Well I am
paying for the cab said Mr S. so I might be allowed to
put my feet were I like.

They traveled 2nd class in the train and Ethel was
longing to go first but thought perhaps least said soon-
est mended. Mr Salteena got very excited in the train
about his visit. Ethel was calm but she felt excited
inside. Bernard has a big house said Mr S. gazing at
Ethel he is inclined to be rich.

Oh indeed said Ethel looking at some cows flashing
past the window. Mr S. felt rarther disheartened so he
read the paper till the train stopped and the porters
shouted Rickamere station. We had better collect our
traps said Mr Salteena and just then a very exalted
footman in a cocked hat and olive green uniform put
his head in at the window. Are you for Rickamere
Hall he said in impressive tones.

Well yes I am said Mr Salteena and so is this lady.

Very good sir said the noble footman if you will
alight I will see to your luggage there is a convayance
awaiting you.

Oh thankyou thankyou said Mr S. and he and
Ethel stepped along the platform. Outside they found
a lovely cariage lined with olive green cushons to
match the footman and the horses had green bridles
and bows on their manes and tails. They got gingerly
in. Will he bring our luggage asked Ethel nervously.

I expect so said Mr Salteena lighting a very long cigar.

Do we tip him asked Ethel quietly.

Well no I dont think so not yet we had better just thank him perlitely.

Just then the footman staggered out with the bagage. Ethel bowed gracefully over the door of the cariage and Mr S. waved his hand as each bit of luggage was hoisted up to make sure it was all there. Then he said thankyou my good fellow very politely. Not at all sir said the footman and touching his cocked hat he jumped actively to the box.

I was right not to tip him whispered Mr Salteena the thing to do is to leave 2/6 on your dressing table when your stay is over.

Does he find it asked Ethel who did not really know at all how to go on at a visit. I beleeve so replied Mr Salteena anyhow it is quite the custom and we cant help it if he does not. Now my dear what do you think of the sceenery.

Very nice said Ethel gazing at the rich fur rug on her knees. Just then the cariage rolled into a beautifull drive with tall trees and big red flowers growing amid shiny dark leaves. Presently the haughty coachman pulled up with a great clatter at a huge front door with tall pillers each side a big iron bell and two very clean scrapers. The doors flung open as if by majic causing Ethel to jump and a portly butler appeared on the scene with a very shiny shirt front and a huge pale face. Welcome sir he exclaimed good naturedly as Mr Salteena alighted rarther quickly from the viacle and please to step inside.

Mr Salteena stepped in as bid followed by Ethel. The footman again struggled with the luggage and the butler Francis Minnit by name kindly lent a hand. The hall was very big and hung round with guns and mats and ancesters giving it a gloomy but a grand air. The butler then showed them down a winding corridoor till he came to a door which he flung open shouting Mr Salteena and a lady sir.

A tall man of 29 rose from the sofa. He was rarther bent in the middle with very nice long legs fairish hair and blue eyes. Hullo Alf old boy he cried so you have got here all safe and no limbs broken.

None thankyou Bernard replied Mr Salteena shaking hands and let me introduce Miss Monticue she is very pleased to come for this visit. Oh yes gasped Ethel blushing through her red ruge. Bernard looked at her keenly and turned a dark red. I am glad to see you he said I hope you will enjoy it but I have not arranged any partys yet as I dont know anybody.

Dont worry murmered Ethel I dont mix much in Socierty and she gave him a dainty smile.

I expect you would like some tea said Bernard I will ring.

Yes indeed we should said Mr Salteena egerly. Bernard pealed on the bell and the butler came in with a stately walk.

Tea please Minnit crid Bernard Clark. With pleshure sir replied Minnit with a deep bow. A glorious tea then came in on a gold tray two kinds of bread and butter a lovly jam role and lots of sugar cakes. Ethels eyes began to sparkle and she made several remarks during the meal. I expect you would now like to unpack said Bernard when it was over.

Well yes that is rarther an idear said Mr Salteena.

I have given the best spare room to Miss Monticue said Bernard with a gallant bow and yours turning to Mr Salteena opens out of it so you will be nice and friendly both the rooms have big windows and a handsome view.

How charming said Ethel. Yes well let us go up replied Bernard and he led the way up many a winding stairway till they came to an oak door with some lovly swans and bull rushes painted on it. Here we are he cried gaily. Ethels room was indeed a handsome compartment with purple silk curtains and a 4 post bed draped with the same shade. The toilit set was white and mouve and there were some violets in a costly varse. Oh I say cried Ethel in supprise. I am glad you like it said Bernard and here we have yours Alf. He opened the dividing doors and portrayed a smaller but dainty room all in pale yellow and wild primroses. My own room is next the bath room said Bernard it is decerated dark red as I have somber tastes. The bath room has got a tip up bason and a hose thing for washing your head.

A good notion said Mr Salteena who was secretly getting jellus.

Here we will leave our friends to unpack and end this Chapter.

The Bread Bin

JOAN AIKEN

This is part of the hilarious tales about Arabel
and her raven, Mortimer, written by one of
today's most popular children's authors.

All the things I am going to tell you now happened
during one terrible, wild, wet week in February,
when Mortimer the raven had been living with the
Jones family in Rumbury Town, London N.W. 3½
for several months. The weather had been so dreadful
for so long that everybody in the family was, if not in
a bad temper, at least less cheerful than usual.

Mrs Jones complained that even the bread felt damp
unless it was made into toast, Arabel had the begin-
nings of a cold, Mr Jones found it very tiring to drive
his taxi through pouring rain along greasy skiddy
roads day after day, and Mortimer the raven was
annoyed because there were two things he wanted to
do, and he was not permitted to do either of them.

He wanted to be given a ride round the garden on Arabel's red truck; Mrs Jones would not allow it because of the weather; and he wanted to climb into the bread bin and go to sleep there. It seemed to him highly unreasonable that he was not allowed to do this.

'We could keep the bread somewhere else,' Arabel said.

'So I buy a bread bin that costs eighty-seven-and-a-half pence for a great, black, sulky, lazy bird to sleep in? What's wrong with the coal-scuttle? He's slept in that for the last three weeks. So it's suddenly not comfortable any more?'

Mrs Jones had just come back from shopping, very wet; she began taking groceries and vegetables out of her wheeled shopping-bag and dumping them on the kitchen floor. She hung her dripping umbrella beside the tea-towels.

'He wants a change,' Arabel said, looking out of the window at the grey lines of rain that went slamming across the garden like telephone wires.

'Oh, naturally! Ginger marmalade on crumpets that bird gets for his breakfast, spaghetti and meatballs for lunch, brandysnaps for supper, allowed to sit inside the grandfather clock whenever he wants, *and* slide down the stairs whenever he feels like it on my best wedding tray painted with pink and green gladioli, and he must have a change as well? That bird gets more attention than the Lord Mayor of Hyderabad.'

'*He* doesn't know that,' Arabel said. 'He's never been to Hyderabad.'

'So could we all do with a change,' said Mrs Jones. 'What's so particular about him that he should get one when the rest of us have to do without?'

Arabel and Mortimer went slowly away into the front hall. After a while Arabel picked up Mortimer, sat him on one of her roller-skates, tied a bit of string to it, and pulled him around the downstairs part of the house. But neither of them cheered up much. Arabel's throat felt tight and tickly. Mortimer knew all the scenery too well to be interested in the trip. He rode along with his head sunk down between his shoulders and his beak sunk down among his chest feathers, and his back and wing feathers all higgledy-piggledy, as if he didn't care which way they pointed.

The telephone rang.

Mortimer meant to get to it first – he loved answering the telephone – but he had one of his long toenails caught in the roller-skate. Kicking and flapping to free himself he started the skate rolling, shot through the hall door, across the kitchen, knocked over Mrs Jones's openwork vegetable rack, which had four pounds of brussels sprouts in the top compartment, and cannoned off that into a bag of coffee beans and a tall container of oven spray, which began shooting out thick frothy foam. Mrs Jones's umbrella fell off the towel-hanger and stabbed clean through a ripe melon which had rolled underneath. A fierce white smoke came boiling off the oven-spray which made everybody cough; Mrs Jones rushed to open the window. A lot of rain and wind blew in, knocking over a tall jar of daffodils that stood on the window-sill; Mortimer, who was interested in putting rough, knobbly things underneath flat, smooth things, began quickly sliding the daffodils (which were made of plastic) underneath the kitchen mat.

'Don't touch that foam!' said Mrs Jones, and she grabbed a large handful of paper towels and mopped it up. The telephone went on ringing.

Mortimer suddenly noticed the open window; he left the daffodils, climbed up the handles of the drawers under the kitchen sink, very fast, claw over claw, scrabbled along the edge of the sink, skated up the draining-board, hoisted himself up on to the sill, and looked out into the wild, wet, windy garden.

'Drat that phone!' said Mrs Jones, mopped up the last of the foam, and rushed to the front hall. Just as she got there, the telephone stopped ringing.

Mortimer, leaning out of the window, saw that Arabel's red truck was down below on the grass, with half an inch of rain inside it. He jumped out.

'Mortimer!' said Arabel. 'Come inside! You'll get wet.'

Mortimer was wet already. He was loving it. He took no notice of Arabel.

There were half a dozen conkers floating in the red truck. The next-door cat, Ginger, was sitting under a holly-bush, trying to keep dry. Mortimer stood in the truck (the water came up to his knee-feathers) and began throwing conkers at Ginger.

'Mortimer!' said Arabel, hanging out of the

window. 'You are not to throw conkers at Ginger. He's never done you any harm.'

Mortimer took no notice. He threw another conker.

Arabel wriggled back off the draining-board, opened the back door, ran out into the wet garden, grabbed the string of the truck, and pulled it back indoors, with Mortimer on board.

A good deal of the water slopped out on to the kitchen floor; it was like a tidal wave carrying the coffee beans and brussels sprouts towards the hall door.

'*Arabel,*' said Mrs Jones, coming back into the kitchen. 'Have you been out of doors in your bedroom slippers? Oh my stars, if you don't catch your mortal end one of these days my name's Mrs Gypsy Petulengro!'

'I had to fetch Mortimer, he was getting wet,' said Arabel. 'I stayed on the path.'

'Getting wet?' Mrs Jones said. 'Why shouldn't he get wet? So you think we should dry him off with the hair-drier? Birds are *meant* to get wet; that's what they have feathers for.'

'Kaaaark,' said Mortimer. He shook his feathers. Drops of rain flew about the kitchen.

Mrs Jones shoved the truck outside, slammed the back door, and began to mop the floor, among the sprouts and the coffee beans.

The phone began to ring again.

Arabel thought the hair-drier was a good idea.

While Mrs Jones hurried off to answer the telephone, Arabel took the hair-drier out of its box, plugged it in, and started blowing Mortimer dry. She put her feet one on each side of him to hold him in place and blew them at the same time, as they were rather cold.

All Mortimer's feathers stood on end, making him look like a turkey. He was so startled that he said, 'Nevermore!' and stepped backwards into a pan of bread rolls that Mrs Jones had set to rise in front of the kitchen fire. He sank into the dough up to his ankles and left a trail of footprints across the pan from corner to corner. But he enjoyed being dried and turned round several times so that Arabel could blow him all over.

'That was Auntie Brenda,' said Mrs Jones, coming back after a long chat. She was in a hurry to finish the mopping and didn't notice Arabel putting away the hair-drier. 'She says she's taking her lot roller-skating at the rink and she'll stop by and pick us up too.'

'Oh,' said Arabel.

'Don't you want to go roller-skating?' said Mrs Jones.

'Well, I expect Mortimer will enjoy it,' said Arabel.

'I just hope he doesn't disgrace us,' said Mrs Jones, giving Mortimer an old-fashioned look. 'But I'm not going out and leaving him alone in the house. Never shall I forget, not if I was to live to eighty and be elected Beauty Queen of the Home Counties, the time we went to *Babes in the Wood* and when we got back he'd eaten the banisters and the bathroom basin complete and two-and-a-half packets of assorted Rainbow Bath Oil Bubble Gums.'

'Nevermore,' said Mortimer.

'Promises, promises,' said Mrs Jones.

'The house looked lovely, all full of bubbles,' Arabel said. 'Mortimer thought so too.'

'Anyway, he's not having the chance to do it again. Put your coat on. Auntie Brenda will be here in ten minutes.'

Arabel put her coat on very slowly. Her throat tickled worse and worse; she did not feel in the least like going out. Also, although they were her cousins, she was not very fond of Auntie Brenda's lot. There were three of them: their names were Lindy, Mindy and Cindy. As a matter of fact, they were horrible girls. They had unkind natures and liked to say things on purpose to hurt other people's feelings. They were always eating, not from hunger but from greed; they thought it was clever to pester their mother into buying them fruit gums and bottles of Coke and bags of crisps and choc-ices all the time they were out. They had more toys than they could be bothered to play with. And they had a lot of spots too.

They had not yet met Mortimer.

Aunt Brenda stopped outside the house in her shiny new car.

Cindy, Lindy and Mindy put their heads out of the window and stopped eating chocolate macaroni sticks long enough to scream:

'Hello, Arabel! We've got new coats, new boots,

new furry hoods, new furry gloves, new skirts and new roller-skates!'

'Spoilt lot,' muttered Mrs Jones, putting Arabel's old roller-skates into her tartan wheeled shopping-bag. 'So what was wrong with the other ones, I should like to know? Anyone would think their dad was president of the Bank of Monte Carlo.'

In fact their dad was a traveller in do-it-yourself wardrobe kits; he travelled so much that he was hardly ever at home.

Arabel went out to the car in her old coat, old hood, old gloves, and old boots. She held Mortimer tightly. He was very interested when he caught sight of the car, his eyes shone like black satin buttons.

'We're going in that car, Mortimer,' Arabel told him.

'Kaaaark,' said Mortimer.

Lindy and Cindy hung out of the back seat window shouting, 'Arabel, Arabel, 'orrible Arabel, 'orrible, 'orrible, 'orrible Arabel.'

Then they spotted Mortimer and their eyes went as round as LP records.

'Coo!' said Lindy. 'What's that?'

'What *have* you got there, 'orrible Arabel?' said Cindy.

'He's our raven. His name's Mortimer,' said Arabel.

All three girls burst into screams of laughter.

'A *raven*? What d'you want a *raven* for? Anyway, he's not a raven – he's just a rusty old rook. He's just a junky old jackdaw. What's the use of him? Can he talk?'

'If he wants to,' said Arabel.

Cindy, Lindy and Mindy laughed even louder.

'I bet all he can say is Caw! See-saw, old Jacky Daw. All he can do is croak and caw!'

'Stop teasing, girls, and make room for Arabel in the back,' said Auntie Brenda.

Arabel and Mortimer got into the back and sat there without saying anything. Cindy started to give Mortimer's tail feathers a tweak, but he turned his head right round on its rusty black neck and looked at her so fiercely that she changed her mind.

Mrs Jones got into the front beside her sister Brenda and they were off.

Mortimer had never ridden in a car before – at least, not when he was conscious. He liked it. As soon as he had made sure that Arabel's cousins were not likely to attack him at once, he began to bounce up and down gently on Arabel's shoulder, looking out at the shops of Rumbury High Street flashing past, at the red buses swishing along, at the street lamps like a string of salmon-coloured daisies, the scarlet letter-boxes and the greengrocers, all red and green and orange and yellow.

'Nevermore,' he muttered. 'Nevermore, nevermore.'

'There, you see,' said Arabel, 'he *can* speak.'

'But what does he mean?' giggled Mindy.

'He means that where he comes from they don't have buses and greengrocers and street lamps and letter-boxes.'

'I don't believe you know what he means at all.'
After that, Arabel kept quiet.

Arabel's three cousins were all expert roller-skaters.
They came to the rink two or three times every week.
They buckled on their new skates and shot off into
the middle, knocking over any amount of people on
the way.

Arabel, when she had put on her skates, went slowly
and carefully round the edge. She did not want to risk
being knocked into, because Mortimer was perched
on her shoulder.

Also she felt very tired, and her throat had stopped
tickling and was now really sore. And her feet were
cold. And her head ached.

'Come on into the middle, cowardy custard! Caw,
caw, cowardy, cowardy!' screamed Lindy and Cindy.

'Yes, go on, ducky, you'll be all right, there's nothing to be afraid of,' called Auntie Brenda. But Arabel
shook her head and stuck to the edge.

Mortimer was having a lovely time. He didn't mind
Arabel's going slowly, because he was so interested in
looking around at all the other skaters. He admired
the way they whizzed in and out and round and
round and through and past and out and in and round.
He dug his claws lovingly into Arabel's shoulder.

'If I had three roller-skates, Mortimer,' said Arabel,
'you could sit on the third one and ride. I wish
I had.'

Mortimer wished it too.

'Tell you what,' said Arabel, 'I'll take my skates off. I don't feel much like skating.'

She sat down at the edge, took her skates off, carried one, and lifted Mortimer on to the other, which she pulled along by the laces.

'Coooo!' shrieked Cindy, whirling past. 'Look at scaredy-baby Arabel, pulling her silly old rook along.'

'Around the ritzy rink the ragged rookie rumbles,' screeched Mindy.

'Scared to skate, scared to skate,' chanted Lindy.

They really were horrible girls.

Arabel went very slowly over to where her mother and Auntie Brenda were sitting.

'Can I go home, please, Ma?' she said. 'My legs ache.'

Mrs Jones looked carefully at her daughter and said, 'Don't you feel well, dearie?'

'No,' said Arabel, and two tears rolled slowly down her cheeks. Mrs Jones put a hand on Arabel's forehead.

'It's hot,' she said. 'I think we'd better go home, Brenda.'

'Oh, dear. The girls *will* be upset.' Brenda raised her voice in a terrific shout. 'Cindy! Lindy! Mi-i-i-ndy! Come along – your cousin's not feeling well.'

Arabel's three cousins came dragging slowly across the rink with sulky expressions.

'*Now* what?' said Mindy.

'We only just got here,' said Cindy.

'Just because 'orrible Arabel can't skate –' said Lindy.

'Ma? Can't you and I go home by bus?' Arabel said.

Auntie Brenda and the three girls looked hopeful at this, but Mrs Jones shook her head again. 'I think we ought to get you home as quickly as possible. Besides, I've left my shopping-bag in the boot of your car, Brenda.'

'Oh, very well,' said Brenda impatiently. 'Come on, girls.'

They took their skates off very slowly and all trailed off to the car-park, which was the multi-storey kind. Aunt Brenda's car was up on the fourth level.

Mortimer was very sorry to leave the rink. He looked back disappointedly as long as the skaters were in sight. But when they came within view of the car-park he cheered up again.

'It's not worth waiting for the lift,' said Auntie Brenda. So they walked up.

Arabel's legs ached worse and worse; Mortimer and the skates, which she was carrying, seemed heavier and heavier. But Mortimer was even more interested by the car-park than he had been by the skating-rink. He gazed round at the huge concrete slopes, and the huge level stretches, and the cars dotted about everywhere, yellow, red, blue, green, black, orange, and silver, like berries on a huge concrete tree.

Mortimer's eyes sparkled like blackcurrant wine gums.

While Auntie Brenda was rummaging for her car key at the bottom of her cluttered handbag, Arabel's arms began to ache so much that she put her skates down on the ground.

With a neat wriggle, Mortimer slid from Arabel's grasp, and climbed on to one of her skates. Then he half spread his wings and gave himself a mighty shove-off. The roller-skate, with Mortimer sitting on it, went whizzing with the speed of a Vampire jet along the flat concrete runway between the two rows of parked cars.

'Oh quick, stop him, stop him!' said Arabel. 'He'll go down the ramp.'

She meant to shout, but the words only came in a whisper.

Lindy, Mindy and Cindy rushed after Mortimer. But they bumped into each other, and were too late to catch him. So he shot down the ramp on to the third level.

'Nevermore, nevermore, nevermore, *nevermore*!' he shouted joyfully, and gave himself another shove with his wings, off a parked Citroën, which sent him up the ramp on the opposite side, and back on to the fourth level.

'There he goes – there!' cried Auntie Brenda. 'Catch him quickly, girls!' But Cindy, Mindy and Lindy were now out of earshot down on the third level.

'Oh good gracious me did you ever see anything so outrageously provoking in all your born *days*?' said Mrs Jones. 'I never did, not even when I worked at the do-it-yourself delicatessen; don't you go running after that black-feathered monster, Arabel, you stay right here.'

But Arabel had gone toiling up after Mortimer to the fifth level.

'Mortimer! Please come back!' she pleaded, in her voice that would not come out any louder than a whisper. '*Please* come back. I don't feel very well. I'll bring you here again another day when the wind's not quite so cold.'

Mortimer didn't hear her.

Up on the fifth level the wind was icy, and whistled like a saw-blade. Arabel began to shiver and couldn't stop.

Mortimer was having a wonderful time, shooting up and down the ramps, in and out between the cars, rowing himself along with his wings at a terrific rate.

Other people, car-owners, began running after him.

'Stop that bird!' shouted Auntie Brenda, and she added angrily to her sister: 'Why you ever wanted to bring him here I really cannot imagine.'

Lots of people were after Mortimer now; but he was going so extremely fast that it was easy for him to dodge them; he had discovered the knack of steering the roller-skate with his tail; he spun round corners and between people's legs and umbrellas and shopping-baskets as if he were entered for the All-Europe Raven Bobsleigh Finals.

After ten minutes there must have been at least fifty

people chasing from one ramp to another, all over and up and down the multi-storey car-park.

In the end, Mortimer was caught quite by chance when a solidly built lady, who had just come in from the outside stairs, spread out her open umbrella to twirl the rain off before closing it; Mortimer, swinging round a Ford Capri on one wheel, ran full tilt into the umbrella and found himself tangled among the spokes. By the time he was untangled Auntie Brenda, very cross, had marched up and seized him by the scruff.

'*Now* perhaps we can get a move on,' she snapped, and carried him kicking back to the car. 'He can go in your shopper, Martha,' she said grimly, 'then he won't be able to give any more trouble. I really don't know why you wanted to come to the roller-skating rink with a *raven*.'

Mrs Jones was too anxious about Arabel to argue.

After five minutes or so, Lindy, Cindy and Mindy came panting and straggling back from the fourth level, and Arabel came shivering back from the fifth.

They all climbed into the car.

As Auntie Brenda drove out of the multi-storey car-park, Arabel felt most peculiar. She just couldn't stop shivering. 'Where's Mortimer?' she whispered.

'He's in the boot and there he'll stay till you get home,' Auntie Brenda said. 'That bird's in disgrace.'

Arabel started to say, 'He didn't know he was doing anything wrong. He thought the car-park was a skating rink for ravens,' but the words stuck inside, as if her throat were full of grit.

By the time they reached the Jones's house, Number Six, Rainwater Crescent, Arabel was crying as well as shivering. She couldn't seem to stop doing either of those things.

Mrs Jones jumped out of the car and almost carried Arabel into the house.

'Your shopper!' Brenda shouted after her, getting the tartan bag out from the boot.

'Put it in the front hall, Brenda.'

Brenda did. But she and Martha had exactly similar tartan shopping-bags on wheels, which they had bought together at a grand clearance sale in Rumbury Bargain Basement Bazaar. Brenda put the wrong shopping-bag in the front hall. She left the one that still contained Mortimer in her car boot. Besides Mortimer, it also held two pounds of ripe bananas. Mortimer, who dearly loved bananas and never got nearly enough of them, was too busy just then to complain about being shut inside the bag.

'We'll get home quick,' Auntie Brenda said. 'We won't hang about in case what Arabel's got is something catching.'

She had to make three stops in any case, on the way home, for Cindy wanted a Dairy Isobar, Lindy wanted a Hokey-Coke and Mindy wanted a bag of Chewy Gooeys; all these things had to be bought at different shops. By the time they reached Auntie Brenda's house, Mortimer had finished the bananas and was willing to be released from the tartan bag.

When Auntie Brenda undid the zip, expecting to

see two raspberry dairy bricks, half a dozen hundred-watt light bulbs, and a head of celery, out shot Mortimer, leaving behind him an utter tangle of empty rinds and squashed banana pulp.

'Oh my dear cats alive!' said Auntie Brenda.

Mortimer was so smothered in banana pulp that for a minute she did not even recognize him. But when she did she cried: 'Girls! It's that awful bird of Arabel's. Quick! Catch the nasty brute. He needs teaching a lesson, that bird does.'

Lindy snatched up a walking-stick, Cindy got a tennis racket, Mindy found a shrimping-net left over from last summer at Prittlewell-on-Sea. They started chasing Mortimer all over their house.

Mortimer never flew if he could help it; he preferred walking at a dignified pace, or, better still, being pulled along on a truck; but just now it seemed best to fly. He found it slightly difficult to open his wings because of all the mashed banana, but he managed it. He flew to the drawing-room mantelpiece. Mindy took a swipe at him with her shrimping-net and knocked off the gilt clock under its glass dome.

Mortimer left the mantelpiece and flew to the light in the middle of the room; he dangled from it upside down like a bat, shaking off particles of banana. Cindy whirled her tennis racket and sent the light bulb, shade and all, smashing through the window. Mortimer had left just before and flown to the top of the bookshelf. Lindy tried to hook him with her walking-stick, but all she did was break a glass pane of the bookshelf door.

'Use your hands, idiots,' shouted Auntie Brenda. 'You're breaking the place up.'

So they dropped their sticks and rackets and nets and went after Mortimer with their hands. Mortimer never, never pecked Arabel. But then she had never pulled his tail, or grabbed him by the leg, or nearly wrenched his wing out of its socket; fairly soon Cindy, Lindy and Mindy were covered with peck-marks and bleeding quite freely here and there.

Auntie Brenda tried throwing a tablecloth over Mortimer. That didn't catch him; she knocked over a table lamp and a jar of chrysanthemums. But, after a long chase, she managed to get him cornered in the fireplace.

The fire was not lit.

Mortimer went up the chimney.

'Now we've got him,' said Auntie Brenda.

'He'll fly out at the top,' said Lindy.

'He can't, there's a cowl on it,' said Cindy.

They could hear Mortimer, scrabbling in the chimney and muttering 'Nevermore,' to himself.

Auntie Brenda telephoned the sweep, whose name was Ephraim Suckett; she asked him to come round right away.

In ten minutes he arrived, full of curiosity, with his long flexible rods, and his brushes, and his huge vacuum cleaner, which looked like a tar barrel with a tube leading out of it.

'Been having a party?' Mr Suckett said, looking round the drawing-room. 'Wonderful larks teenagers get up to.'

'We've got a bird in the chimney,' said Auntie Brenda. 'I want you to get him out as soon as you can.'

'A bird, eh?' said Mr Suckett cautiously, looking at the damage. 'He wouldn't be one o' them Anacondors with a wing-spread of twenty foot? If so I want extra cover in advance under my Industrial Injuries Policy.'

'He's an ordinary common raven,' snapped Auntie Brenda. 'Please get him out quickly. I want to light the fire. My husband will be home soon.'

So Mr Suckett poked one of his rods up the chimney as far as it would go, and then screwed another on to the bottom end and poked that up, and then screwed another one on to *that*. The rods bent like liquorice. A lot of soot fell into the hearth.

'When did you last have this chimney swept?' Mr Suckett asked. 'Coronation year?'

Mortimer retired further up the chimney.

Meanwhile, what had happened to Arabel?

She had gone to hospital.

Mrs Jones rang the doctor as soon as she was indoors. The doctor came quickly and said that Arabel had a nasty case of bronchitis, she would be better off in Rumbury Central, so Mr Jones, who had just come home, drove her there at once in his taxi, wrapped up in three pink blankets with her feet on a hot-water bottle.

'Where's Mortimer? Is he all right?' whispered Arabel in the taxi. 'What about his tea?'

'Father will give him his tea when he gets home

after leaving us,' said Mrs Jones. Mrs Jones was allowed to stay with Arabel.

She had clean forgotten about Mortimer being inside the tartan shopping-bag.

Mr Jones left his wife and daughter at the hospital, and drove home slowly and sadly. He put his taxi away in its shed. In the front hall he found a tartan shopping-bag containing two raspberry dairy bricks, some light bulbs and a head of celery. He ate the celery and put the other things away. 'Wonder why Martha got all those bulbs?' he thought. 'She must know there's a dozen already in the tool cupboard.'

Still hungry, even after the celery, he made himself a pot of tea and a large dish of spaghetti in cheese sauce, which was the only thing he knew how to cook.

Then, suddenly, it struck him that the house was unusually quiet. Normally, when Mortimer was about, there would be a scrunching, or a scraping, or a tapping, or a tinkling, as the raven carefully took something to pieces, or knocked something over to see if it would break, or chewed it to see if it was chewable, or pushed one thing underneath some other thing.

'Mortimer?' called Mr Jones. 'Where are you? What are you doing? Stop whatever it is, and come here.'

No answer. Nobody said 'Nevermore.' The house remained silent.

Mr Jones began to feel anxious. Although not a man to make a fuss of people, he was fond of Mortimer. Also he wanted to be quite sure the raven was not eating the back wall of the house, or digging a hole under the boiler, or unravelling the bath towels (Mortimer could take a whole bath towel to pieces in three-and-a-half minutes flat, leaving ten miles of snaggled yarn draped over the floor), or munching up the *Home Handyman's Encyclopaedia* in ten volumes. Or anything else.

High and low, Mr Jones hunted over the whole house for Mortimer, and didn't find him anywhere.

'Oh my dear cats,' he thought, 'the bird must have wandered out unbeknownst while we were getting Arabel into the taxi with the pink blankets. She will be upset when she hears he's gone. How shall we ever be able to break it to her? She thinks the world of that bird.'

Just then the telephone rang.

When Mr Jones lifted the receiver off its rest, words came out of it in a solid shriek.

'What's that?' said Mr Jones, listening. 'Who is that? This is Jones's Taxi Service, Rumbury Town. *Brenda?* Is that you? Is something the matter?'

The shriek went on. All Mr Jones could distinguish was something about chrysanthemums, and something about soot, and something about a clock.

'Soot in the clock,' he thought, 'that's unusual. Maybe they've got an oil-fired clock, I dare say such things do exist, and Brenda's always been dead keen on having everything very up to date. I can't help you, Brenda, I'm afraid,' he said into the telephone. 'I

don't know much about oil-fired clocks; matter of
fact I don't really know anything at all; you'll have to
wait till Arthur gets home. We're all at sixes and
sevens here because Arabel's gone to hospital.'

And he rang off; he felt he had more things to
worry about than soot in his sister-in-law's clock.

Meanwhile, what had been happening to Mortimer?

Mr Suckett the sweep had fastened all his rods together
and poked them up Auntie Brenda's chimney. Mortimer
had retired right to the very top; but he could not get
out. It was possible to see out though through the slits of
the cowl, and he found the view very interesting, for the
house was right on top of Rumbury Hill. Mortimer
could see for miles, over Rumbury Heath, down across
London as far as the Houses of Parliament.

Mr Suckett's rods were not quite long enough to
dislodge Mortimer; Auntie Brenda's chimney was unusually high.

Discovering this, Mr Suckett began pulling his rods
down again, and unscrewing them one by one.

'What'll you do now?' asked Lindy.

'Will you have to take the top of the chimney off?'
asked Mindy.

'Shall we light a fire and toast him?' said Cindy.

'Just get rid of him *somehow* and be quick about it,'
said Auntie Brenda.

'We'll have to suck him out,' said the sweep.

He withdrew the last of his rods, and wheeled his
vacuum cleaner close up to the fireplace.

This cleaner was like an ordinary household one, but about eight times larger, with eight times as powerful a suck. It had a big canvas drum on wheels, into which all the soot was sucked down the tube. When he had finished a chimney-sweeping job, Mr Suckett wheeled the drumful of soot away, and sold the soot to people at fifty-nine pence a pound, to put on their slugs. Better than orange peel, he said it was.

By now the canvas drum was packed to bursting with all the soot that had been in Auntie Brenda's chimney, piling up since Coronation year.

Mr Suckett shoved the nozzle of the long tube right up the chimney and switched on the motor.

It had a tremendously powerful suck. It could yank a St Bernard dog right off its feet and up a ten-foot ramp at an angle of thirty degrees against a force-six wind. It sucked Mortimer down the chimney like one of his own feathers.

He shot down backwards, along the canvas tube, and ended up inside the canvas drum, stuffed in with a hundredweight of soot.

Mortimer had quite enjoyed being in the chimney where, if dark, it was interesting, besides there had been that pleasant view from the top.

But he did not at all enjoy being sucked down so fast – backwards and upside down too – still less did he like being packed into a bag full of suffocating black powder.

He began to kick and flap and peck and shout 'Nevermore'. In less time than it takes to tell, he had jabbed and clawed a huge hole in the side of the canvas drum; he burst through this hole like a black bombshell, and a hundredweight of soot followed him out.

Auntie Brenda had opened all the windows when Mr Suckett began poking his rods up the chimney; she said the smell of soot made her faint; Mortimer went out through a window with the speed of a Boeing 707; he had had enough of Auntie Brenda's house.

He left a scene of such blackness and muddle behind him that I do not really think it would be worth trying to describe it.

Mortimer did not fly very far; he really disapproved of flying. As soon as he was in the street he glided down to the ground and set off walking. He had no idea where Auntie Brenda's house was, nor where Arabel's house was, but this did not worry him. Since Auntie Brenda's house was on the top of a hill he walked downhill, and he studied each front door as he passed it, in case it was the right one. None were. He walked very slowly.

Mr Jones was just going to start eating his spaghetti, and wondering if he should call up the hospital to ask how Arabel was getting on, when the telephone rang.

It was Mrs Jones.

'Is that you, Ben?' she said. 'Oh dear, Ben, Arabel's ever so ill, tossing and turning and deliriated, and she keeps asking for Mortimer and the doctor says it will be all right for you to bring him as the sight of him might do her good.'

Mr Jones's heart fell into his sheepskin slippers.

'But Mortimer's not here,' he said.

'Not *there*? Whatever do you mean, Ben, he must be there?'

Then, for the first time Mrs Jones remembered and let out a guilty gulp. 'Oh bless my soul whatever will I forget next? I quite forgot that poor bird, though gracious knows the bother he caused with the coffee beans and the car-park and throwing conkers at Ginger who never touched a feather of his tail (not but what he would if he could I dare say). Anyhow a couple of hours shut up in a bag won't have done him any harm but no more than he deserves for all his troublesomeness, anyway you better let him out right away, poor thing.'

'Let him out of *where*?'

'My zip tartan shopping-bag. He's inside it.'

'No he's not, Martha,' said Mr Jones. 'There was a head of celery, two family dairy bricks, and half a dozen hundred-watt bulbs. What did you want to get *them* for? There's lots in the tool cupboard.'

Mrs Jones let out another squawk. 'Oh my stars, then he must be at Brenda's! She must have left the wrong bag. I hope those girls of hers aren't teasing him. You'd better go right round there and fetch him, Ben, and bring him to the hospital, and bring two more of Arabel's nighties, can you, and a packet of tea-bags and my digestive mint lozenges.'

'Round at Brenda's, is he?' Mr Jones said slowly. A lot of things began to make sense to him, the soot and the chrysanthemums and the clock. 'All right, Martha, I'll go and fetch him and bring him to you as soon as I can.'

He did not mention to Martha about the clock and the chrysanthemums; she had enough to worry about already. He rang off, then dialled Brenda's number.

There was no reply. In fact the line seemed to be out of order; Mr Jones could hear a kind of muffled sound at the other end, but that was all.

It wasn't hard to guess that if there had been any trouble at Brenda's house, then Mortimer the raven was somehow connected with that trouble.

Mr Jones scratched his head. Then he took off his slippers and put on his shoes and overcoat again. Sighing, he drove his taxi out of its shed, turned right, and went up to where Rainwater Crescent meets Rumbury High Street. This is quite a busy junction and there are four traffic-lights, or should be; this evening they did not seem to be working.

The traffic was in a horrible tangle. Two policemen were trying to sort it out, and a third was inspecting, with the help of a big torch, the chewed stumps like celery-ends that were all that was left of the Rainwater junction lights.

'Evening, Sid,' said Mr Jones, putting his head out of the cab window. 'What's up, then?'

'That you, Ben? Well, you'll think I'm barmy, but someone seems to have eaten the traffic-lights.'

'Oh,' said Mr Jones.

He reflected. Then he did a U-turn – luckily there was nobody behind him – and drove down the crescent again. Twenty yards further down he got out of the cab.

'Mortimer?' he called. 'Where are you?'

'Nevermore,' said a voice at ankle-level in the dark behind him. Although he had been expecting something of the kind, Mr Jones jumped. Then he turned round, and saw Mortimer, with his eyes shining in the light of the street lamps, walking slowly along by the hedge, peering in at all the front gates of the houses as he came to them. He was on the wrong side of the street, so it was likely that he would have passed clean by Number Six and gone on goodness knows where.

Mr Jones picked him up. Mortimer was never a light bird but at the moment, with two pounds of bananas inside him, he weighed as much as the London Telephone Directories with the classified section as well.

'I dare say I ought to hand you over to the police for eating the traffic-lights and causing an obstruction,' Mr Jones said severely, 'but Arabel's ill in hospital so I'm going to take you to see her first, we'll worry about the other things tomorrow. And you'd better behave yourself in the hospital; they won't stand for any tricks there.'

'Kaaaark,' said Mortimer. Mr Jones was not absolutely encouraged by the way he said it. But there was no time to go into a lot of explanations about hospitals; besides, it was unlikely that Mortimer would listen.

Mr Jones hurried home to pack up the nightdresses, tea bags and digestive peppermint lozenges. While he was doing this, Mortimer wandered into the kitchen and saw the large dish of spaghetti that Mr Jones had cooked for his supper.

'Nevermore,' he said sadly. He walked all round the dish, studying it from every side.

Mortimer loved spaghetti in cheese sauce, it was one of his favourite between-meals snacks, but just at the moment he was so full of bananas that he found himself unable to eat a single string.

Even if he couldn't eat the spaghetti, though, he didn't want to let it go to waste. He looked for a box, jar, or container to put it in; when allowed to do so, Mortimer would stay happy and busy for quite a long time, packing spaghetti into yoghurt pots or egg boxes or whatever happened to be at hand.

He had just tidied away the last of the spaghetti when Mr Jones hurried back with the mints and nightdresses, grabbed a box of tea-bags from the kitchen cupboard, dropped all these things into the tartan zip bag, put on his overcoat again, and picked up Mortimer.

He did not notice that the spaghetti dish was empty.

By now it was quite late at night, but Mr Jones supposed that it would be all right to go to the hospital, even though it was after visiting hours, since the doctor had told him to bring Mortimer.

He drove his taxi to Rumbury Central, parked in

the big front forecourt, and walked inside with Mortimer on his shoulder.

Mortimer was amazed by the hospital. He liked it even better than the multi-storey car-park. It had been built about a hundred years ago by Florence Nightingale, of black-pudding coloured brick. It was huge, like a prison; several of its corridors were about a mile long. The ceilings were so high that the echoes from the smallest sound, even sounds out in the street, were as loud as thunder. Many patients believed that nurses and doctors were allowed to drive cars along the corridors, but this was not actually the case.

Mr Jones went up to the fourth floor in a great creaking lift as big as a post office. Mortimer said 'Kaark,' because the lift reminded him of Rumbury Town Station. They walked along miles of green-floored passage until they found Balaclava Ward.

When they reached the door there was nobody in sight to tell Mr Jones whether he was allowed to go in. But there were two large windows like portholes in the doors, so Mr Jones stood on tiptoe, with Mortimer on his shoulder, and peered through.

He could see a double row of white-covered beds, six on each side, and half-way along, his wife Martha, sitting by one of them. He caught her eye and waved; she made signs that he was to wait until the Sister – who wore a white pie-frill cap and sat at a desk near the door – noticed him and let him in.

Mr Jones nodded to show he understood.

He stuck his hands in his pockets and prepared to wait quietly.

But he didn't wait quietly. Instead he let out a series of such piercing yells that patients shot bolt upright in their beds all over that part of the hospital, porters rammed their trolleys into doors, nurses dropped whole trays of instruments, and doctors swallowed the ends of their stethoscopes.

Mortimer, who had been sitting very quiet and interested, looking about him, flew straight up into the air and circled round and round, flapping his wings and shouting, 'Nevermore, *nevermore!*'

Mr Jones fainted dead away on the floor.

Sister Bridget Hagerty came rushing out of the ward. She was small and black-haired and freckled; her eyes were as blue as blue scouring-powder; when she gave orders for a thing to be done, it was done right away. But everybody liked her.

'What in the name of goodness is going on here?' she snapped.

Dr Antonio arrived. He was in charge of that part of the hospital at night; he had just come on duty. He was not the doctor who had told Mrs Jones to have Mortimer brought along; in fact Dr Antonio couldn't stand birds. He had been frightened by a tame cockatoo at the age of three, in his pram; ever since then, the sight of any bird larger than a bluetit brought him out in a rash.

He came out in a rash now, bright scarlet, at sight of Mortimer.

'It's obvious what's going on!' he said. 'That great black brute has attacked this poor fellow. Palgrave! Where are you? Come here, quick!'

Palgrave was the ward orderly. He had gone off to fetch the doctor a cup of instant coffee. He came running along the corridor.

'Palgrave, get that bird out of here, quickly!'

'Yes sir, right away, sir,' said Palgrave, and he opened the landing window and threw the cup of hot coffee all over Mortimer, who was still circling round up above, wondering what was the matter with Mr Jones.

Mortimer didn't care for coffee unless it was very sweet, and his feelings were hurt; he flew straight out of the window.

'Doctor, there's something very funny about this man,' said Sister Bridget, who was kneeling down by Mr Jones. 'Why do you suppose his hands are all covered with spaghetti in cheese sauce?'

'Perhaps he's a burn case, an emergency,' suggested the doctor. 'Perhaps he couldn't find anything else and so he used the spaghetti as a burn dressing. We had better take him along to Casualty. Palgrave, get a stretcher.'

'But his pockets are full of spaghetti too,' said Sister Bridget.

'Perhaps he was on his way to visit some Italian friends,' said the doctor. 'Perhaps he *is* Italian. *Parla Italiano?*' he shouted hopefully into Mr Jones's ear.

Mr Jones groaned.

'Parla Italiano?' said the doctor again.

Mr Jones, who had flown over Italy as a pilot in World War II, said feebly, 'Have we crashed? Where's my rear gunner? Where's my navigator?'

'A mental case,' said Dr Antonio. 'Speaks English, hands covered in spaghetti, asks for his navigator; without doubt, a mental case. Palgrave, fetch a strait-jacket.'

Palgrave put down the stretcher he had just brought and went off again.

Luckily at this moment Mrs Jones came out of Balaclava Ward, wondering what was going on, and what had become of Ben. When she saw him lying on the ground, his hands covered in spaghetti, she let out a gasp.

'Oh, Ben, dear! What ever has been happening?'

'Do you know this man, Mrs Jones?' asked Sister Bridget.

'It's my husband! What's happened?'

'He seems to have fainted,' said the Sister.

Mr Jones came to a bit more. 'Is that you, Martha?' he said faintly. 'Worms. Worms in my pocket. It was the shock –'

'Oh my goodness gracious I should think so, what-ever next?' cried his wife. 'Worms in your pocket, how did they come to be there, then?'

'It wasn't worms, it was spaghetti,' said Sister Bridget, helping Mr Jones to sit up and fanning him with the strait-jacket Palgrave had brought. 'Could you fetch a cup of tea, please, Palgrave? How did you come to have your pockets full of spaghetti, Mr Jones?'

'Instant coffee, instant stretcher, instant strait-jacket, instant tea,' grumbled Palgrave, stomping off again.

'Spaghetti? Oh, that must have been Mortimer, it's just like his naughty ways,' said Mrs Jones. 'Last time I left him alone with a bowl of spaghetti for five minutes he packed the whole bowlful in among my Shetland knitting wool. Arabel's friends were asking where she got her spaghetti-Fair Isle sweater for weeks after. *Ben!* Where *is* Mortimer?'

Mr Jones struggled to his feet and drank the cup of tea Palgrave had just brought.

'Mortimer? Isn't he here? He was here just now. Have you seen a raven?' he asked Palgrave.

'Raven? Big black hairy bird? I chucked him out the window with a cup of Whizzcaff over his tail feathers,' said Palgrave. 'Doc there told me to.'

'Oh, no!' wailed Mrs Jones. 'Dr Plantagenet said the medicine didn't seem to be having any effect and a sight of Mortimer was the one thing that might make Arabel feel better.'

She looked beseechingly at the Sister. Sister Bridget looked at Palgrave. Palgrave looked at the doctor, who looked at his feet.

'Better go outside and start hunting for him, and quick about it,' said the Sister.

'Instant coffee, instant strait-jacket, instant tea,

instant raven,' grumbled Palgrave, and followed the doctor out through the fire door on to the fire escape. It was raining hard, and very dark indeed.

The Dog That Bit People

JAMES THURBER

James Thurber was an American humorist,
much of whose work first appeared in period-
icals like the *New Yorker*. Like Edward Lear he
did drawings too. Dorothy Parker, a famous
American journalist, said that his people have
'the semblance of unbaked cookies', and he
was particularly good at portraying hopelessly
dim-looking dogs.

Probably no one man should have as many dogs in
his life as I have had, but there was more pleasure
than distress in them for me except in the case of an
Airedale named Muggs. He gave me more trouble
than all the other fifty-four or five put together, although my moment of keenest embarrassment was
the time a Scotch terrier named Jeannie, who had just
had six puppies in the clothes closet of a fourth floor
apartment in New York, had the unexpected seventh

and last at the corner of Eleventh Street and Fifth Avenue during a walk she had insisted on taking. Then, too, there was the prize-winning French poodle, a great big black poodle – none of your little, untroublesome white miniatures – who got sick riding in the rumble seat of a car with me on her way to the Greenwich Dog Show. She had a red rubber bib tucked around her throat and, since a rain storm came up when we were half-way through the Bronx, I had to hold over her a small green umbrella, really more of a parasol. The rain beat down fearfully and suddenly the driver of the car drove into a big garage, filled with mechanics. It happened so quickly that I forgot to put the umbrella down and I will always remember, with sickening distress, the look of incredulity mixed with hatred that came over the face of the particular hardened garage man that came over to see what we wanted, when he took a look at me and the poodle. All garage men, and people of that intolerant stripe, hate poodles with their curious hair cut, especially the pom-poms that you have got to leave on their hips if you expect the dogs to win a prize.

But the Airedale, as I have said, was the worst of all my dogs. He really wasn't my dog, as a matter of fact: I came home from a vacation one summer to find that my brother Roy had bought him while I was away. A big, burly, choleric dog, he always acted as if he thought I wasn't one of the family. There was a slight advantage in being one of the family, for he didn't bite the family as often as he bit strangers. Still, in the years that we had him he bit everybody but Mother, and he made a pass at her once but missed. That was during the month when we suddenly had mice, and Muggs refused to do anything about them. Nobody ever had mice exactly like the mice we had that month. They acted like pet mice, almost like mice somebody had trained. They were so friendly that one night when Mother entertained at dinner the Friraliras, a club she and my father had belonged to for twenty years, she put down a lot of little dishes with food in them on the pantry floor so that the mice would be satisfied with that and wouldn't come into the dining-room. Muggs stayed out in the pantry with the mice, lying on the floor, growling to himself – not at the mice, but about all the people in the next room that he would have liked to get at. Mother slipped out into the pantry once to see how everything was going. Everything was going fine. It made her so mad to see Muggs lying there, oblivious of the mice – they came running up to her – that she slapped him and he slashed at her, but didn't make it. He was sorry immediately, Mother said. He was always sorry, she said, after he bit someone, but we could not understand how she figured this out. He didn't act sorry.

Mother used to send a box of candy every Christmas to the people the Airedale bit. The list finally contained forty or more names. Nobody could understand why we didn't get rid of the dog. I didn't understand it very well myself, but we didn't get rid of him. I think that one or two people tried to poison

Muggs – he acted poisoned once in a while – and old Major Moberly fired at him once with his service revolver near the Seneca Hotel in East Broad Street – but Muggs lived to be almost eleven years old and even when he could hardly get around, he bit a Congressman who had called to see my father on business. My mother had never liked the Congressman – she said the signs of his horoscope showed he couldn't be trusted (he was Saturn with the moon in Virgo) – but she sent him a box of candy that Christmas. He sent it right back, probably because he suspected it was trick candy. Mother persuaded herself it was all for the best that the dog had bitten him, even though Father lost an important business association because of it. 'I wouldn't be associated with such a man,' Mother said, 'Muggs could read him like a book.'

We used to take turns feeding Muggs to be on his good side, but that didn't always work. He was never in a very good humour, even after a meal. Nobody knew exactly what was the matter with him, but whatever it was it made him irascible, especially in the mornings. Roy never felt very well in the morning, either, especially before breakfast, and once when he came downstairs and found that Muggs had moodily chewed up the morning paper, he hit him in the face with a grapefruit and then jumped up on the dining-room table, scattering dishes and silverware and spilling the coffee. Muggs's first free leap carried him all the way across the table and into a brass fire screen in front of the gas grate, but he was back on his feet in a moment and in the end he got Roy and gave him a pretty vicious bite in the leg. Then he was all over it; he never bit anyone more than once at a time. Mother always mentioned that as an argument in his favour; she said he had a quick temper but that he didn't hold a grudge. She was forever defending him. I think she liked him because he wasn't well. 'He's not strong,' she would say, pityingly, but that was inaccurate; he may not have been well but he was terribly strong.

One time my mother went to the Chittenden Hotel to call on a woman mental healer who was lecturing in Columbus on the subject of 'Harmonious Vibrations'. She wanted to find out if it was possible to get harmonious vibrations into a dog. 'He's a large tan-coloured Airedale,' Mother explained. The woman said that she had never treated a dog, but she advised my mother to hold the thought that he did not bite and would not bite. Mother was holding the thought the very next morning when Muggs got the iceman, but she blames that slip-up on the iceman. 'If you didn't think he would bite you, he wouldn't,' Mother told him. He stomped out of the house in a terrible jangle of vibrations.

One morning when Muggs bit me slightly, more or less in passing, I reached down and grabbed his short stumpy tail and hoisted him into the air. It was a foolhardy thing to do and the last time I saw my mother, about six months ago, she said she didn't know what possessed me. I don't either, except that I was pretty mad. As long as I held the dog off the floor by his tail he couldn't get at me, but he twisted and jerked so, snarling all the time, that I realized I couldn't hold him that way very long. I carried him to the kitchen and flung him on to the floor and shut the door on him just as he crashed against it. But I forgot about the backstairs. Muggs went up the backstairs and down the frontstairs and had me cornered in the living-room. I managed to get up on to the mantelpiece above the fireplace, but it gave way and came down with a tremendous crash throwing a large marble clock, several vases, and myself heavily to the floor. Muggs was so alarmed by the racket that when I picked myself up he had disappeared. We couldn't find him anywhere, although we whistled and shouted, until old Mrs Detweiler called after dinner that night. Muggs had bitten her once, in the leg, and she came into the living-room only after we assured her that Muggs had run away. She had just seated herself when, with a great growling and scratching of claws, Muggs emerged from under a davenport where he had been quietly hiding all the time, and bit her again. Mother examined the bite and put arnica on it and told Mrs Detweiler that it was only a bruise. 'He just bumped you,' she said. But Mrs Detweiler left the house in a nasty state of mind.

Lots of people reported our Airedale to the police, but my father held a municipal office at the time and was on friendly terms with the police. Even so, the cops had been out a couple of times – once when Muggs bit Mrs Rufus Sturtevant and again when he bit Lieutenant-Governor Malloy — but Mother told them that it hadn't been Muggs's fault, but the fault of the people who were bitten. 'When he starts for them, they scream,' she explained, 'and that excites him.' The cops suggested that it might be a good idea to tie the dog up, but Mother said that it mortified him to be tied up and that he wouldn't eat when he was tied up.

Muggs at his meals was an unusual sight. Because of the fact that if you reached towards the floor he would bite you, we usually put his food plate on top of an old kitchen table with a bench alongside the table. Muggs would stand on the bench and eat. I remember that my mother's Uncle Horatio, who boasted that he was the third man up Missionary Ridge, was splutteringly indignant when he found out that we fed the dog on a table because we were afraid to put his plate on the floor. He said he wasn't afraid of any dog that ever lived and that he would put the dog's plate on the floor if we would give it to him. Roy said that if Uncle Horatio had fed Muggs on the ground just before the battle, he would have been the first man up Missionary Ridge. Uncle Horatio was furious. 'Bring him in! Bring him in now!' he shouted. 'I'll feed the — on the floor!' Roy was all for giving him a chance, but my father wouldn't hear of it. He said that Muggs had already been fed. 'I'll feed him again!' bawled Uncle Horatio. We had quite a time quieting him.

In his last year Muggs used to spend practically all

of his time outdoors. He didn't like to stay in the house for some reason or other – perhaps it held too many unpleasant memories for him. Anyway, it was hard to get him to come in and as a result the garbage man, the iceman, and the laundryman wouldn't come near the house. We had to haul the garbage down to the corner, take the laundry out and bring it back, and meet the iceman a block from home. After this had gone on for some time, we hit on an ingenious arrangement for getting the dog in the house so that we could lock him up while the gas meter was read, and so on. Muggs was afraid of only one thing, an electrical storm. Thunder and lightning frightened him out of his senses (I think he thought a storm had broken the day the mantelpiece fell). He would rush into the house and hide under a bed or in a clothes closet. So we fixed up a thunder machine out of a long narrow piece of sheet iron with a wooden handle on one end. Mother would shake this vigorously when she wanted to get Muggs into the house. It made an excellent imitation of thunder, but I suppose it was the most roundabout system for running a household that was ever devised. It took a lot out of Mother.

A few months before Muggs died, he got to 'seeing things'. He would rise slowly from the floor, growling low, and stalk stiff-legged and menacing towards nothing at all. Sometimes the Thing would be just a little to the right or left of a visitor. Once a Fuller Brush salesman got hysterics. Muggs came wandering into the room like Hamlet following his father's ghost. His eyes were fixed on a spot just to the left of the Fuller Brush man, who stood it until Muggs was about three slow, creeping paces from him. Then he shouted. Muggs wavered on past him into the hallway, grumbling to himself, but the Fuller man went on shouting. I think Mother had to throw a pan of cold water on him before he stopped. That was the way she used to stop us boys when we got into fights.

Muggs died quite suddenly one night. Mother wanted to bury him in the family lot under a marble stone with some such inscription as 'Flights of angels sing thee to thy rest' but we persuaded her it was against the law. In the end we just put up a smooth board above his grave along a lonely road. On the board I wrote with an indelible pencil 'Cave Canem'. Mother was quite pleased with the simple classic dignity of the old Latin epitaph.

The Balaclava Story

GEORGE LAYTON

The author of this story is not only a funny writer, he's a funny actor too. You may remember him as Des in *Minder* or as Bombardier Solomons in *It Ain't Half Hot, Mum* on the television. He's written several stories based on his own northern childhood and this one is probably the best known.

Tony and Barry both had one. I reckon half the kids in our class had one. But I didn't. My mum wouldn't even listen to me.

'You're not having a balaclava! What do you want a balaclava for in the middle of summer?'

I must've told her about ten times why I wanted a balaclava.

'I want one so's I can join the Balaclava Boys . . .'

'Go and wash your hands for tea, and don't be so silly.'

She turned away from me to lay the table, so I put the curse of the middle finger on her. This was pointing both your middle fingers at somebody when they weren't looking. Tony had started it when Miss Taylor gave him a hundred lines for flicking paper pellets at Jennifer Greenwood. He had to write out a hundred times: 'I must not fire missiles because it is dangerous and liable to cause damage to someone's eye.'

Tony tried to tell Miss Taylor that he hadn't fired a missile, he'd just flicked a paper pellet, but she threw a piece of chalk at him and told him to shut up.

'Don't just stand there – wash your hands.'

'Eh?'

'Don't say "eh", say "pardon".'

'What?'

'Just hurry up, and make sure the dirt comes off in the water, and not on the towel, do you hear?'

Ooh, my mum. She didn't half go on sometimes.

'I don't know what you get up to at school. How do you get so dirty?'

I knew exactly the kind of balaclava I wanted. One just like Tony's, a sort of yellowy-brown. His dad had given it to him because of his earache. Mind you, he didn't like wearing it at first. At school he'd given it to Barry to wear and got it back before home-time. But, all the other lads started asking if they could have a wear of it, so Tony took it back and said from then on nobody but him could wear it, not even Barry. Barry told him he wasn't bothered because he was going to get a balaclava of his own, and so did some of the other lads. And that's how it started – the Balaclava Boys.

It wasn't a gang really. I mean they didn't have meetings or anything like that. They just went around together wearing their balaclavas, and if you didn't have one you couldn't go around with them. Tony and Barry were my best friends, but because I didn't have a balaclava, they wouldn't let me go round with them I tried.

'Aw, go on, Barry, let us walk round with you.'

'No, you can't. You're not a Balaclava Boy.'

'Aw, go on.'

'No.'

'Please.'

I don't know why I wanted to walk round with them anyway. All they did was wander up and down the playground dressed in their rotten balaclavas. It was daft.

'Go on, Barry, be a sport.'

'I've told you. You're not a Balaclava Boy. You've got to have a balaclava. If you get one, you can join.'

'But I can't, Barry. My mum won't let me have one.'

'Hard luck.'

'You're rotten.'

Then he went off with the others. I wasn't half fed up. All my friends were in the Balaclava Boys. All the lads in my class except me. Wasn't fair. The bell went for the next lesson – ooh heck, handicraft with the

Miseryguts Garnett – then it was home-time. All the Balaclava Boys were going in and I followed them.

'Hey, Tony, do you want to go down the woods after school?'

'No, I'm going round with the Balaclava Boys.'

'Oh.'

Blooming Balaclava Boys. Why wouldn't *my mum* buy *me a balaclava*? Didn't she realize that I was losing all my friends, and just because she wouldn't buy me one?

'Eh, Tony, we can go goose-gogging – you know, by those great gooseberry bushes at the other end of the woods.'

'I've told you, I can't.'

'Yes, I know, but I thought you might want to go goose-gogging.'

'Well, I would, but I can't.'

I wondered if Barry would be going as well.

'Is Barry going round with the Balaclava Boys an' all?'

'Course he is.'

'Oh.'

Blooming balaclavas. I wish they'd never been invented.

'Why won't your mum get you one?'

'I don't know. She says it's daft wearing a balaclava in the middle of summer. She won't let me have one.'

'I found mine at home up in our attic.'

Tony unwrapped some chewing-gum and asked me if I wanted a piece.

'No thanks.' I'd've only had to wrap it in my handkerchief once we got in the classroom. You couldn't get away with anything with Mr Garnett.

'Hey, maybe you could find one in your attic.'

For a minute I wasn't sure what he was talking about.

'Find what?'

'A balaclava.'

'No, we haven't even got an attic.'

I didn't half find handicraft class boring. All that mucking about with compasses and rulers. Or else it was weaving, and you got all tangled up with balls of wool. I was just no good at handicraft and Mr Garnett agreed with me. Today was worse than ever. We were painting pictures and we had to call it 'My favourite story'. Tony was painting *Noddy in Toyland*. I told him he'd get into trouble.

'Garnett'll do you.'

'Why? It's my favourite story.'

'Yes, but I don't think he'll believe you.'

Tony looked ever so hurt.

'But honest. It's my favourite story. Anyway what are you doing?'

He leaned over to have a look at my favourite story.

'Have you read it, Tony?'

'I don't know. What is it?'

'It's *Robinson Crusoe*, what do you think it is?'

He just looked at my painting.

'Oh, I see it now. Oh yes, I get it now. I couldn't

make it out for a minute. Oh yes, there's Man Friday behind him.'

'Get your finger off, it's still wet. And that isn't Man Friday, it's a coconut tree. And you've smudged it.'

We were using some stuff called poster paint, and I got covered in it. I was getting it everywhere, so I asked Mr Garnett if I could go for a wash. He gets annoyed when you ask to be excused, but he could see I'd got it all over my hands, so he said I could go, but told me to be quick.

The washbasins were in the boys' cloakroom just outside the main hall. I got most of the paint off and as I was drying my hands, that's when it happened. I don't know what came over me. As soon as I saw that balaclava lying there on the floor, I decided to pinch it. I couldn't help it. I just knew that this was my only chance. I've never pinched anything before – I don't think I have – but I didn't think of this as . . . well . . . I don't even like saying it, but . . . well, stealing. I just did it.

I picked it up, went to my coat, and put it in the pocket. At least I tried to put it in the pocket but it bulged out, so I pushed it down the inside of the sleeve. My head was throbbing, and even though I'd just dried my hands, they were all wet from sweating. If only I'd thought a bit first. But it all happened so quickly. I went back to the classroom, and as I was going in I began to realize what I'd done. I'd *stolen* a balaclava. I didn't even know whose it was, but as I stood in the doorway I couldn't believe I'd done it. If only I could go back. In fact I thought I would but then Mr Garnett told me to hurry up and sit down. As I was going back to my desk I felt as if all the lads knew what I'd done. How could they? Maybe somebody had seen me. No! Yes! How *could* they? They could. Of course they couldn't. No, of course not. What if they did though? Oh heck.

I thought home-time would never come, but when the bell did ring I got out as quick as I could. I was going to put the balaclava back before anybody noticed; but as I got to the cloakroom, I heard Norbert Lightowler shout out that someone had pinched his balaclava. Nobody took much notice, thank goodness, and I heard Tony say to him that he'd most likely lost it. Norbert said he hadn't, but he went off to make sure it wasn't in the classroom.

I tried to be all casual and took my coat, but I didn't dare put it on in case the balaclava popped out of the sleeve. I said tarah to Tony.

'Tarah, Tony, see you tomorrow.'

'Yes, tarah.'

Oh, it was good to get out in the open air. I couldn't wait to get home and get rid of that blooming balaclava. Why had I gone and done a stupid thing like that? Norbert Lightowler was sure to report it to the Headmaster, and there'd be an announcement about it at morning assembly and the culprit would be asked to own up. I was running home as fast as I could. I wanted to stop and take out the balaclava and chuck it away, but I didn't dare. The faster I ran, the faster my head was filled with thoughts. I could give it back to Norbert. You know, say I'd taken it by mistake. No, he'd never believe me. None of the lads would believe me. Everybody knew how much I wanted to be a Balaclava Boy. I'd have to get rid of the blooming thing as fast as I could.

My mum wasn't back from work when I got home, thank goodness, so as soon as I shut the front door, I put my hand down the sleeve of my coat for the balaclava. There was nothing there. That was funny, I was sure I'd put it down that sleeve. I tried down the other sleeve, and there was still nothing there. Maybe I'd got the wrong coat. No, it was my coat all right. Oh, blimey, I must've lost it while I was running home. I was glad in a way. I wasn't going to have to get rid of it, now it was gone. I only hoped nobody had seen it drop out, but, oh, I was glad to be rid of it. Mind you, I was dreading going to school next morning. Norbert'll probably have reported it by now. Well, I wasn't going to own up. I didn't mind the cane, it wasn't that, but if you owned up, you had to go up on the stage in front of the whole school. Well I was going to forget about it now and nobody would ever know that I'd pinched that blooming lousy balaclava.

I started to do my homework, but I couldn't concentrate. I kept thinking about assembly next morning. What if I went all red and everybody else noticed? They'd know I'd pinched it then. I tried to think about other things, nice things. I thought about bed. I just wanted to go to sleep. To go to bed and sleep. Then I thought about my mum; what she'd say if she knew I'd been stealing. But I still couldn't forget about assembly next day. I went into the kitchen and peeled some potatoes for my mum. She was ever so pleased when she came in from work and said I must've known she'd brought me a present.

'Oh, thanks. What've you got me?'

She gave me a paper bag and when I opened it, I couldn't believe my eyes – a blooming balaclava.

'There you are, now you won't be left out and you can stop making my life a misery.'

'Thanks, Mum.'

If only my mum knew she was making *my* life a misery. The balaclava she'd bought me was just like the one I'd pinched. I felt sick. I didn't want it. I couldn't wear it now. If I did, everybody would say it was Norbert Lightowler's. Even if they didn't, I just couldn't wear it. I wouldn't feel it was mine. I had to get rid of it. I went outside and put it down the lavatory. I had to pull the chain three times before it went away. It's a good job we've got an outside lavatory or else my mum would have wondered what was wrong with me.

I could hardly eat my tea.

'What's wrong with you? Aren't you hungry?'

'No, not much.'

'What've you been eating? You've been eating sweets, haven't you?'

'No, I don't feel hungry.'

'Don't you feel well?'

'I'm all right.'

I wasn't, I felt terrible. I told my mum I was going upstairs to work on my model aeroplane.

'Well, it's my bingo night, so make yourself some cocoa before you go to bed.'

I went upstairs to bed, and after a while I fell asleep. The last thing I remember was a big balaclava, with a smiling face, and it was the Headmaster's face.

I was scared stiff when I went to school next morning. In assembly it seemed different. All the boys were looking at me. Norbert Lightowler pushed past and didn't say anything. When prayers finished I just stood there waiting for the Headmaster to ask for the culprit to own up, but he was talking about the school fête. And then he said he had something very important to announce and I could feel myself going red. My ears were burning like anything and I was going hot and cold both at the same time.

'I'm very pleased to announce that the school football team has won the inter-league cup . . .'

And that was the end of assembly, except that we were told to go and play in the schoolyard until we were called in, because there was a teachers' meeting. I couldn't understand why I hadn't been found out yet, but I still didn't feel any better. I'd probably be called to the Headmaster's room later on.

I went out into the yard. Everybody was happy because we were having extra playtime. I could see all

the Balaclava Boys going round together. Then I saw
Norbert Lightowler was one of them. I couldn't be
sure it was Norbert because he had a balaclava on, so I
had to go up close to him. Yes, it was Norbert. He
must have bought a new balaclava that morning.

'Have you bought a new one then, Norbert?'

'Y'what?'

'You've bought a new balaclava, have you?'

'What are you talking about?'

'Your balaclava. You've got a new balaclava,
haven't you?'

'No, I never lost it at all. Some fool had shoved it
down the sleeve of my raincoat.'

Daisy Parker's Funerals
from *Bagthorpes V. the World*

HELEN CRESSWELL

Daisy Parker is the Bagthorpes' four-year-old cousin. She has already gone through a Fire Phase (including setting fire to her sandpit at playschool) and her Flood Phase. She has an invisible friend called Arry Awk, who tends to get the blame for anything that goes wrong . . .

It later transpired that Daisy had now entered a new Phase. Uncle Parker called it a Morbid Phase, but Aunt Celia insisted that it was an Intimations of Mortality Phase. Under whatever label, what it meant, principally, was that Daisy was now holding funerals. Sometimes she held only one a day, at other times several. It depended mainly on what she could find to

bury. She took these ceremonies very seriously, and tried as far as possible to dress for her part. On the present occasion, for instance, she had taken advantage of the disorganization in the kitchen to bear off a long Indian frock of Mrs Bagthorpe's that was airing on a rail, and a striped tea-towel. She was swathed in the frock and wore the towel on her head. She said that she thought her outfit looked religious, and that vicars always wore long frocks.

What Daisy was burying no one thought to inquire at the time, as the ceremony was almost complete when they all rushed out to see what was happening. They stopped more or less in their tracks at the sight of Daisy in her borrowed vestments. She was scattering earth into a small hole and had real tears running down her face. There could be little doubt that this new Phase was a serious one.

'Goodbye, goodbye!' she wailed, flinging the last fistfuls of earth into the grave. 'Where are you gone now, poor little fing?'

This question struck her audience as rhetorical, and no one attempted to offer a reply.

'Darling child!' cried Aunt Celia, and she swayed forward to embrace her daughter, thereby collecting a good deal of damp soil on her own frock, and inciting Mr Bagthorpe's further wrath.

'Ye gods!' he exclaimed in disgust. 'What more must I endure? That child, Russell, is in urgent need of treatment. You are mad. She is mad.' Then, after a pause, 'They are mad.'

He was declining the verb to deaf ears.

'Come, Daisy,' Grandma said. 'You must not be upset. Come to my room, and you shall have some sugared almonds.'

Daisy instantly disengaged herself from her mother's embrace.

'I can't come, Grandma Bag,' she cried. 'I've got to do the *writing* yet.'

The writing was in fact one of the parts of her burials that Daisy enjoyed most. It meant composing a fitting epitaph for each of her various victims. She was very original in her choice of monuments, as the Bagthorpes were later to discover to their cost. Mr Bagthorpe said that the people who ran Highgate Cemetery could learn a lot from her. On this occasion she had appropriated a black non-stick baking sheet from Mrs Fosdyke's cupboard, and intended to chalk on it.

'You'll have to go away,' she told them all. 'I can't fink and write poems when there's people there.'

On this first occasion, no one has a clue what Daisy is burying. When the Bagthorpes do find out, they are not amused . . .

'Where did you say you'd put that chicken?' Mrs Fosdyke's voice broke into Mrs Bagthorpe's self-congratulatory reverie.

'What? Oh – the chicken. Surely – on the side, Mrs Fosdyke.'

She rose.

'At least, I think . . .' she eyed dubiously the empty work-top. 'I may have put it in the fridge, later . . . we had rather a trying day yesterday. Now where . . .?'

She stooped to examine the contents of the refrigerator.

'Extraordinary . . .' she murmured. Mrs Fosdyke had gone back into the pantry.

'Not in 'ere!' she called. 'Found it, 'ave you?'

'No. No, I have not,' admitted Mrs Bagthorpe. 'But the whole thing is quite absurd. I removed the chicken from the deep freeze, I placed it – I placed it somewhere *here* . . . and then . . .' her voice trailed away. She really had no inkling of the bird's movements beyond this juncture.

Mr Bagthorpe then entered, followed closely by Jack and William.

'Ah, Henry!' his wife greeted him. 'Perhaps you can throw some light on the matter.'

'What matter?' he demanded ungraciously.

'Mrs Fosdyke and I have mislaid a chicken,' she told him.

'And what, Laura, in the name of all that is wonderful, do you suppose *I* would do with a chicken?' he asked her.

'Well – nothing, of course, dear,' she faltered. 'I simply thought . . .'

'Simply nothing,' came the terse rejoinder. 'In this house, nothing is simple.'

'No, dear, of course not. But it *is* all such a mystery. You see, I moved this chicken from the deep freeze, and I placed it –'

'When?' interrupted William. He, in company with Jack, was more interested in the whereabouts of the missing chicken than was their father. They had both dreamed of it, a gravied oasis in a desert of lettuce and beetroot.

'Yesterday morning.' She was becoming a little desperate. 'I remember it quite distinctly. You may have noticed it standing on the side yourself, Mrs Fosdyke?'

'I might've,' Mrs Fosdyke said non-committally. 'I can't say I remember.'

'But I did, I definitely did,' Mrs Bagthorpe insisted. 'I *mentioned* it, you may remember?'

'You mentioned it, all right,' Jack told her reassuringly. 'You said you were going to put it in a casserole.'

'That's right! There!' she cried gratefully.

Her husband favoured her with a cool stare.

'Then where *have* you put it, Laura?' he inquired. 'Could it be that you have casseroled it already, and forgotten?'

'Oh Henry, do be *serious*!' Mrs Bagthorpe tried at all times to keep her sense of perspective, but could feel it now blurring into virtual invisibility.

'Let's do a recap,' William intervened. 'Reconstruct the thing. You took the chicken out in the morning. Right?'

'Right,' his mother agreed.

'And Mrs Fosdyke did not witness this, so at present we have only your word for it. Mrs Fosdyke went home.'

'I never asked to!' Mrs Fosdyke put in loudly.

'We then had lunch. As we finished, Uncle Parker came.'

'And Aunt Celia. *And* Daisy,' Jack said.

There was a sudden chill pause.

'*And* Daisy,' Jack repeated.

'Who held a funeral,' William supplied in flat tones. He sat down suddenly.

'But *surely* . . .?' Mrs Bagthorpe faltered. 'Oh – I'm sure you are wrong!'

Followed closely by Jack, she hurried to the outer door, to Mrs Fosdyke's extreme mystification.

Jack and his mother stood and stared at Daisy's epitaph, chalked on to a non-stick black baking sheet:

> Higledy pigledy pore ded hen
> Yore fethers will nevver cum back agen.
> 1763–1800

Jack read this inscription out loud, to convince himself.

'Oh my God!' Mr Bagthorpe was now behind them. 'Even unto the grave!'

William and Mrs Fosdyke had now joined them round the newly dug grave.

'Whatever . . .? That's my best non-stick baking –!' Mrs Fosdyke snatched up the monument and began to wipe off the inscription with her wraparound pinafore. Jack, oddly, found himself fleetingly shocked by this desecration.

'So our dinner is under there, we can take it?' said Mr Bagthorpe unnecessarily. There could be no escaping this conclusion.

'The bird was, after all, dead,' said Mrs Bagthorpe feebly, 'and to the child it must have seemed the most natural thing in the world to bury it. She was weeping, Henry.'

'*I* am almost weeping,' he informed her, unmoved by this reminder of his niece's tenderheartedness. 'I shall telephone Russell at once.'

He left the graveside, cursing under his breath. It occurred to Jack that while it had been his father's idea to follow a policy of eating spring onions and rhubarb, he could hardly have been looking forward to this, any more than anybody else. The casseroled chicken must have appeared to him, too, a welcome landmark in such a diet.

'You mean to say,' came the disbelieving voice of Mrs Fosdyke (who did not, after all, know that Daisy had gone into a new Phase of Intimations of Mortality), 'that that Daisy's dug that bird into the *soil*?'

'I – I fear so, Mrs Fosdyke,' Mrs Bagthorpe told her faintly. 'But we must try not to be too harsh in our judgement. The bird was, after all, dead, and must have appeared to her –'

'You've already said that, Mother,' said William coldly. What he really wished was that the hen was in the casserole, and Daisy in the grave.

'I don't believe –!' came Mrs Fosdyke's voice flatly. 'Here!' She bent, and began to scrabble at the earth with her fingers.

'Ugh!' she screeched, and fell back.

Gleaming through the disturbed soil was the nude, pale pink and mottled skin of what was, unmistakably, an oven-ready chicken.

Mrs Bagthorpe shuddered. Even Jack felt as if he would never be able to face a cooked chicken again. He had never thought of one as a *corpse* before. He, too, wished Daisy dead and buried.

Mrs Fosdyke stood stockstill, goggling with shock.

'I don't believe it!' she said at last. And then, genuinely mystified, 'That Daisy – wherever does she get her ideas?'

'I don't know, Mrs Fosdyke,' replied Mrs Bagthorpe truthfully. 'She is certainly a most original child.'

'Original!' Mrs Fosdyke was disgusted.

'Original *and* tiresome,' qualified Mrs Bagthorpe, though Jack could see that from Mrs Fosdyke's point of view, even this description came nowhere near doing justice to the case.

'It'll have to *stop* buried, that is certain,' remarked Mrs Fosdyke. 'And what'll you be having with the veg, Mrs Bagthorpe? And it's to be hoped that dog of yours don't go ferreting down there and dragging chickens with soil on into my kitchen.'

'He won't,' Jack promised. 'He doesn't like digging things up.'

When the news of Daisy's latest exercise in

creativity spread to the rest of the household, feelings ran high. Only Grandma, possibly feeling secure in the prospect of a Fortnum and Mason hamper, seemed unmoved by it.

'Celia has unwittingly produced a genius,' she told the others. 'You had better look to your laurels.'

Daisy herself was very upset by the hostile reaction to her funeral, and about having her gravestone removed and wiped.

'Poor little dead fing!' she sobbed. 'He was all cold and pimply and no feathers. Nobody cares!'

This was not strictly true. The Bagthorpes did care, deeply. Attitudes towards Daisy hardened further. To be ranged up against the whole world was in itself a considerable prospect, but now, it appeared, there was a saboteur within their very walls. The outlook ahead was bleak.

Great Aunt Lucy from Torquay comes to stay. Mr Bag-thorpe goes to the station to meet her . . .

It was very unfortunate that one of Rosie's hamsters was found dead immediately after Mr Bagthorpe's departure. It was William who made this discovery. He had gone into one of the disused stables in search of a length of cable, and his eye chanced to fall on the cages in which the hamsters were kept. He looked at them because at the time they were producing a notice-able degree of noise. Several of the hamsters were busy exercising themselves by running non-stop on their wheels. William, whose mind was currently occupied with devising methods of producing free electricity, cast a thoughtful eye upon them.

'A treadmill,' he murmured to himself. 'A windmill generates electricity, and so could a treadmill. If we could devise a means of harnessing the energy expended by the hamsters in treading those wheels, then we –'

He was halted on the threshold of a scientific breakthrough by observing a limp and furry shape to the fore of one of the cages. He advanced to investigate.

His half-formed theory was nipped in the bud. Clearly hamsters were not up to treading treadmills on any full-time, regular basis. This one had obviously died of a heart attack after its exertions.

'Better tell Rosie,' he decided.

He did so without taking due thought. He might have known, he told himself bitterly later, that Rosie would go straight to tell Daisy of the death by misadventure. Rosie truly loved Daisy, and thought her sweet and funny, and used every means in her power to lure her away from Grandma's side whenever possible.

The result was that Mr Bagthorpe, later in the morning, motoring sedately up the drive with Aunt Lucy beside him, came close to a head-on collision with a funeral procession. It consisted of Daisy wearing a trailing black crocheted shawl and felt hat of Grandma's, followed by Rosie and Grandma herself, both suitably attired in deep mourning, and carrying flowers. It had been Grandma's idea to inter the hamster in the front garden, rather than the back, because she had secretly hoped for the confrontation that in fact now took place. She was exceedingly pleased with this outcome. It established herself in the eyes of the visitor as dauntingly and possibly unbeatably eccentric, and it goaded Mr Bagthorpe into a towering rage. Round one, Grandma thought with satisfaction, had definitely gone to her.

Mr Bagthorpe had to pull up quite sharply to avoid a situation that would have involved at least one real funeral, if not three. Jack heard the gravel scatter, and approached cautiously behind the screen of laurels to observe the scene. He looked first, naturally, at Great Aunt Lucy, to see if she would be how he had imagined her. In fact, her face was the least noticeable thing about her, sandwiched as it was between a large beflowered hat, and a chest crowded with lace and a good number of shining ornaments. (These later turned out to be brooch watches, all set at different times.)

The most striking figure present was undoubtedly Grandma, who was wearing a black bonnet and veil that she had kept for nearly half a century in case she ever wanted to take up bee-keeping again. None of her features were even faintly discernible under this thick veil, and Jack wondered how she could see where she was going. Rosie had struck a more casual note in a black leotard and tights, but evidently thought the

addition of a hat necessary to the solemnity of the
occasion, and wore low over her eyes a greenish-black
homburg, presumably the property of Grandpa.

The members of this procession were singing a kind
of dirge, or even three separate dirges. When Mr
Bagthorpe wound down his window and started shouting they were not deflected from their course. They
appeared to give only the briefest of glances in his
direction, and then made slowly off over the far lawn,
presenting an eerie picture in the brilliant midday sun.
Jack himself was torn between following the car to
the house, and attending the funeral. He decided on
the latter course. A funeral was less of an everyday
occurrence than the spectacle of Mr Bagthorpe shouting.

He caught up with the cortège just as it halted by
what was clearly to be the final resting place of Rosie's
hamster. Daisy was carrying a chocolate box. She
placed it reverently under a lilac bush, and Jack guessed
that it contained the corpse. She then delved under
her layers of shawl and skirts and produced a trowel.

'You better sing another verse while I'm digging,'
she told the other mourners, and herself set to work in
a businesslike way with the trowel. A hole soon materi-
alized.

'Now,' said Daisy with satisfaction. 'Now it's the
proper part. Oh dear, poor little mouse!'

'Hamster,' Rosie told her, sniffing. 'His name was
Truffles.'

Daisy held aloft the chocolate box for a moment, in

the manner of a magician inviting an audience to inspect a receptacle from which he is about to produce a dozen white doves.

'Goodbye, Truffles!' she said. Tears were already beginning to roll down her cheeks. Evidently a long personal relationship with the deceased was not necessary in order for her to experience deep feelings of bereavement.

'There you go now, for ever and ever, down into the soil for ever and ever!'

She bent and placed the box in the hole.

'Ashes to ashes, dusters to dusters,' she cried loudly, scattering handfuls of soil over the coffin.

Jack was unable to judge the strength of Grandma's emotions behind her black curtain, but Rosie was by now sobbing in earnest. She herself moved in and threw some soil.

'Goodbye, Truffles,' she sobbed.

'Poor dead Truffles,' agreed Daisy. 'For ever and ever,' she added, evidently feeling that these words had a strong ecclesiastical ring.

The hole filled in, Daisy straightened up.

'Now we'll sing hymn four thousand and ninety-six,' she announced. '"We Plough the Fields and Scatter."'

Jack thought this choice curious, but supposed that Daisy had only a limited repertoire of hymns. Her congregation obediently struck up, and Jack thought how amazing it was that Grandma should be so docile and allow Daisy to take the leading role. Usually if

Grandma was involved in anything, she insisted on running it.

The trio sang nearly half 'We Plough the Fields and Scatter' before they trailed off for lack of words.

'Amen,' Daisy said. 'That'll do. Now we've got to do the flowers and writing.'

She again delved into her robes and produced what looked like a large, slender volume, with a message printed on it in yellow. This she pushed at something of an angle into the soil at the head of the grave.

'I seen books in the graveyard,' Daisy told the others. 'Books are good. Now put the flowers on.'

Grandma and Rosie then advanced with their bunches of flowers and each in turn placed her tribute under the headstone.

'For ever and ever amen,' Daisy said, terminating the ceremony. 'We better go and have dinner now. Goodbye, poor dead mouse.'

'Hamster,' Rosie told her again.

Jack waited until the mourners had disappeared from sight, then advanced to inspect the grave. The headstone, he noted with misgivings, was Mr Bagthorpe's Road Atlas. It bore the inscription:

> Here lies a mous
> In a holey hous
> But the pore ded thing
> Will here the bels ring
> 1692–1792
> Forevver and evver.

'That's oil paint she's used,' Jack thought. 'It'll never come off. Father'll kill her.'

Daisy, having tasted the heady delight of holding funerals, is unstoppable. The trouble is that in the average household corpses are not easy to come by. The Bagthorpes have to compromise . . .

'But what about corpses?' objected Rosie. 'We haven't got any corpses.'

They sat and pondered this incontrovertible truth. Corpses were not, they realized, easily come by, even at Unicorn House.

'Where's she been getting her corpses up to now?' Jack asked. 'Uncle Park said she'd had about two dozen funerals last week. She can't have found two dozen corpses. She must've been burying other things as well.'

'That chicken . . .' William murmured thoughtfully. 'That was dead meat, all right . . .'

'Dead meat!' Jack was struck by a thought. 'Chops and things – out of the deep freeze!'

They considered this proposition. Whether or not Daisy would be moved to bury chops they were not certain. What they did know, was that once the supply of meat in the deep freeze was exhausted, Mr Bagthorpe had ruled that no more was to be purchased. Meat, therefore, was now at a premium. Thoughtful consideration was necessary. Things had to be weighed and balanced.

'What it amounts to,' William said, 'is whether a chop in the grave is worth two in a freezer.'

'Or vice versa,' Tess added.

'I think Daisy *could* bury chops,' Jack told the others. 'She's really dotty about burying things. I think we ought to egg her on.'

'A non-stop procession of funerals would certainly have a depressive effect on Aunt Lucy,' Tess said. 'What we could also do, is turn the conversation as much as possible to the subject of Time.'

This, too, was considered to be a sound proposition. Everyone undertook to do some rifling through books of poetry during spare moments, in search of apt quotations.

'And I'll have a quick scan through the hymn books,' William volunteered. 'Anything about Time in them is usually pretty depressing.'

Jack and Rosie were deputed to catch Daisy during one of the rare moments when she was not in Grandma's room with Little Tommy, and make an effort to rekindle her apparently waning interest in funerals.

'Lay it on really thick,' William advised them. 'Say *you'll* go to the funerals. Tell her I've got a big bell, and'll toll it for her, if she likes. Tell her anything. And don't call the chops chops.'

'Why?' Rosie asked. 'What shall we call them, then?'

'Call them "poor little dead lambs",' he told her. 'Or piglets, as the case may be.'

'Will she be burying *sausages*?' Jack could not see even Daisy looking on these in the light of deceased piglets, and shedding tears over them.

'Pork *chops*, idiot!' William said. 'And while you're digging, keep your eyes open for anything dead. Or any odd bones.' (Daisy, he knew, had a powerful attraction toward skeletons, and had once tried to engineer William into becoming one himself.)

The younger Bagthorpes, then, scattered on their various missions, though these had to be dovetailed with their duties allotted by Mr Bagthorpe on his hell-bent career towards Self-Sufficiency. Currently, Tess was working on the salad section of the garden, Rosie acting as mate to William, who was converting the summer house to a hen house, and Jack just digging.

It was just after lunch (or supper, as Great Aunt Lucy preferred to call it) that Jack and Rosie managed to corner Daisy. They coaxed her into the sitting-room as she was on her way to fetch the kitten for an outing in the garden.

'I can't stop long,' she told them. 'Little Tommy mews when I'm not there.'

'The thing is, Daisy, we need your help,' Jack told her.

'What to do?' she asked. 'I'm not digging. I don't like digging. Except graves,' she added as an after-thought.

Rosie and Jack exchanged triumphant glances. Clearly Daisy was *not* out of her Intimations of Mortality Phase, and her undertaking urges were merely lying dormant.

'That's exactly what it is, Daisy,' Rosie told her. 'A grave. Poor little dead lamb.'

'Little dead lamb?' Daisy's eyes stretched. 'Where? Oh dear, poor little fing!'

Jack knew that the chop was going to prove something of an anticlimax for Daisy, who would be expecting something white and woolly, and accordingly chose his words carefully.

'It has been cut up, I'm afraid,' he told her.

'Oh *dear*!' squealed Daisy, aghast and enchanted at once. 'Oh, *poor* little fing! Oh, when shall we bury him?'

'As soon as you like,' Jack said. 'We'll come to the funeral as well, won't we, Rosie?'

'And Grandma Bag,' Daisy said happily. 'And will old Auntie Lucy come?'

'I shouldn't think so,' Rosie began, but Jack interrupted.

'That's a good idea. You ask her, Daisy.'

The more Great Aunt Lucy heard about Daisy's funerals, the better.

'I'll go and ask her.' Daisy trotted to the door. 'And I'll tell Grandma Bag. You go and get the poor dead lamb. I never buried a lamb before. I'll write him a lovely pome.'

From there on, things rapidly began to snowball. William had already abstracted several chops and other cuts of meat from the deep freeze, and these were defrosting in his room. He had enough potential corpses, he said, to keep Daisy going for days, if necessary.

'Though the sooner Aunt Lucy clears off the better,' he added. 'I'd give anything for a lamb chop with mint sauce.'

They all would. Meals, on Mr Bagthorpe's instructions, were becoming increasingly spartan. He too, it appeared, wished his elderly relative elsewhere.

Daisy invited Great Aunt Lucy to the funeral, but she strenuously declined.

'She said I mustn't *mention* poor dead fings.' Daisy told the rest indignantly as they assembled for the funeral of the chop. 'Silly old griffin!'

Daisy was, as had been anticipated, somewhat disappointed at the lack of resemblance of the chop to a real dead lamb, but soon perked up when she saw the increased number of mourners, and was informed that a bell would toll.

'And I'll take some photos,' Rosie promised.

William had selected a suitable spot for the interment, in full view of Great Aunt Lucy's window. She had gone up to her room for a doze because, she had informed them all at lunch, the full moon was now imminent. Mrs Fosdyke had a prolonged fit of choking when she heard this.

'I shall require some heavier curtains, Laura,' Great Aunt Lucy had continued. 'The present ones are quite inadequate. The rays of the moon will pass straight through them. I am already beginning to be affected by them.'

Mrs Bagthorpe had looked quite desperate at this, and Jack longed to tell her that her fears were groundless, because the old lady would almost certainly have left before the full moon.

Aunt Lucy was wakened, as had been intended, by the loud tolling of William's bell, and Jack, glancing up, saw her inadequate curtains move, and caught a glimpse of her face.

The funeral went swimmingly. Daisy, once she had accepted the fact that her corpse was dismembered, acted as bereaved as she ever had. A further funeral took place several hours later, and she wept at that, too.

'Poor dead piglet, poor dead piglet!' she sobbed as the pork chop was laid in its shallow grave. 'Dusters to dusters, ashes to ashes!'

The younger Bagthorpes themselves found that they, too, were enjoying the proceedings, though they sometimes had difficulty in disguising their giggles as sobs, and Tess was in fact reproved for this on one occasion.

'You *never* laugh at funerals,' Daisy told her severely. 'You *cry*. Jus' try to fink of the poor dead lamb. How would *you* like to be a poor dead lamb?'

A relentless procession of chops, then, made their way to the grave, and a curious assortment of headstones sprang up in the part of the garden designated as the graveyard. Daisy was running out of things large enough for her to write her epitaphs on, so had now adopted the policy of selecting articles for their ornamental value, and then attaching her poems on sheets of paper either sellotaped or pinned on. There was a cross formed by a ruler and silver spoon taped together, a brass candlestick, a pair of cast iron Punch and Judy doorstops and a large Staffordshire figure which, Daisy said, reminded her of an angel.

She was increasingly exercised in the composition of suitable epitaphs, because all her corpses at present fell into only two categories.

'I'm getting *bored* writing pomes jus' about lambs and piglets,' she said, as she attached her latest composition to Mr Bagthorpe's shooting stick. 'I wish I could bury something different. For ever and ever amen.'

The epitaph read:

> All the lams are dying
> All the lams are ded
> Evryone is crying
> Cos the lams has gone to bed.
> Forever and evver.
> 1629–1842

This seemed to Jack to have a more than usually final ring to it. Daisy's boredom threshold was notoriously low. He intensified his search for something more out of the way for her to work on. In the meantime, William told her that one of the chops was a cow, and another a giraffe, it being unlikely that Daisy would see through this fraud.

★

*Daisy's real triumph is the funeral of her imaginary friend,
Arry Awk. This is Grandma's idea . . .*

'Why, dear, do we not hold another funeral, and bury
Arry Awk?'

She had imagined this an inspired thought, and was
not prepared for the violence of Daisy's reactions to
it.

'He isn't dead, he's not, he's not!' she squealed.
'He's my bestest friend in the whole world and he's
not dead! And *he* han't got a wrinkly face and short
legs. He's not *never* going to die, not till I do!'

Most present felt that the time for this double
demise could not come too soon. Grandma, however,
alarmed by the strength of the passions she had
aroused, immediately tried to modify her position.

'Hush, dear,' she told her protégée. 'You have quite
misunderstood me. I was not for a moment suggesting
that Arry Awk was dead. I merely thought that he
might enjoy attending his own funeral.'

Daisy's sobs abated, and you could see that she was
attracted by this novel proposition.

'There are, after all,' Grandma continued cunningly,
'few people who can ever have done this. In fact,
Arry Awk is the only person I have ever known of
who *could* attend his own funeral. It would be an
historic occasion.'

At this Mr Bagthorpe made a strangled noise and
left the room.

'It's all hopeless,' William said gloomily. 'He doesn't

even believe that Aunt Lucy talks about Time all the time and is eternally grateful to us. Can't we get him to go and see for himself?'

'I think that would be most unwise,' his mother said hastily. 'We must give him Time. He must be allowed to work through this obsession with Survival.'

The Bagthorpes sat morbidly contemplating this prospect, and at that moment there came the sound of grinding gravel that meant Uncle Parker had arrived.

'It's Daddy, it's Daddy!' Daisy squealed. '*He* can come to Arry Awk's funeral as well. *Everybody* can,' she added generously. 'And even Uncle Bag, even if he is a nasty Grook!'

Uncle Parker breezed in, accompanied by Aunt Celia.

'Hello, all,' he greeted them. 'Still Surviving, I see?'

'Only just,' William told him.

Aunt Celia passionately embraced Daisy who, as usual, struggled to get free.

'Listen, listen!' she cried. 'We going to have a big funeral today and it's going to be Arry Awk's! And Grandma Bag says it'll be *hysterical*!'

'By Jove!' Uncle Parker was clearly impressed. 'Arry Awk, then, has finally kicked the bucket. I feared we should never see the day. Congratulations, Daisy – or rather, of course, condolences. Think, Laura, Henry and I will be able to reduce our Insurance Premiums which were, one is bound to admit, becoming crippling.'

'No no no!' shrieked Daisy, infuriated that Arry Awk, just because he was going to have a funeral, should be presumed dead. 'He's *not* dead, he's not!'

'Really?' Uncle Parker was quite nonplussed. His daughter's Intimations of Mortality were apparently taking a devious turn. He was slightly shocked. 'We are going to bury him *alive*?'

Obviously he felt that even Arry Awk did not deserve this fate.

'No!' squealed Daisy. 'You're not *listening*! *You* tell him, Mummy! We're going to have a funeral for Arry Awk and he's going to *come* to it!'

Aunt Celia instantly renewed her attempts to embrace Daisy. Evidently she alone perfectly understood the situation.

'It is wonderful!' she told everybody. 'The symbolism of the ceremony is almost too deep for words. We are to witness the Phoenix arising from the ashes!'

'Will it be a cremation, then?' Jack asked. He, for one, devoutly hoped that it would not. This could mean that Daisy would then be in *three* Phases at once, which was a mind-blowing prospect.

'So literal,' murmured Aunt Celia, meaning Jack. 'How rare and precious it is to see poetry in a little child. I am constantly being reminded of how I have, in Daisy, a being quite unique.'

There was nothing in this last statement with which anybody could quarrel, and nobody did.

'Even Little Tommy can come,' Daisy was now burbling. 'You come and see my little pussy now,

Mummy and Daddy. He's getting bigger and bigger and got *ever* so long claws.'

The funeral of Arry Awk took place with due pomp and ceremony. It had been postponed with the arrangement of this pomp and ceremony in mind. Most people attended in the end, optimistically imagining that this was a finale, the *pièce de résistance* to mark the end of Daisy's Phase of Intimations of Mortality. Even Uncle Parker went. You never knew, he said, Arry Awk might accidentally fall into his own grave, and that he would not want to miss.

In the event, he was not far short of the truth. To begin with, things went smoothly enough. Daisy trotted round her procession inspecting its members and making sure everyone was wearing some black and carrying a floral tribute. She herself was bearing a bunch of flowers and foliage almost as big as herself, tied with pink ribbon and having a card attached that read 'Goodby Arry Awk my bestest frend in the hole world for evver and evver amen'. She had also appropriated her most original monument to date, in the shape of a giant glass jar of green bubble bath which would serve, she said, to remind Arry Awk of his lovely flood. His epitaph she had already composed in private, and intended to attach it with ribbon to the neck of the jar at the end of the ceremony.

She had insisted that Arry Awk be buried away

from what was by now known as the Highgate Cemetery end of the garden. She was probably dimly aware that, even in death, Arry Awk was something on his own.

'It is as though,' crooned Aunt Celia dotingly, 'the darling child has unconsciously recognized the need for a Poet's Corner.'

Mr Bagthorpe elected, predictably, to give the funeral a miss, even though Daisy had magnanimously said he could attend. William, too, was absent, there being no possibility of later disinterring Arry Awk and having *him* with mint sauce. He was not even prepared to toll the bell, so Rosie volunteered for this duty. Unfortunately, she had not acquired the knack of tolling a handbell, and the resulting sound was more like a summons to school dinner than a solemn call to mourning. The vibrations of this clanging got on everybody's nerves in the end, with the astonishing exception of Aunt Celia, who, one would have imagined, would have been the first to clap her hands over her ears.

'No man is an island entire unto himself,' she was heard to murmur. And 'Never send to know for whom the bell tolls, it tolls for thee.'

She was presumably somewhere so far off on her own that she was not even hearing the vibrations, let alone feeling them.

The spot Daisy had selected for the laying to rest of the imaginary remains of Arry Awk was at the edge of the shrubbery, near a flowering rhododendron.

(This imaginary side of things was very confusing to everybody except Daisy herself, and her mother. So far as the Bagthorpes were concerned, Arry Awk had always been imaginary and invisible, and it was weird the way Daisy seemed to think he was imaginarily in the empty toffee tin, but actually in pride of place in the procession at her side.)

'Come on, Arry Awk,' she said, instituting the proceedings, 'you jus' walk along with me. Walk in slow steps, and don't talk – jus' sing.'

The cortège set off, wailing in a dirge-like way. Daisy had said they could all sing anything they liked, so long as it was sad. Simultaneously and mercifully the bell stopped tolling, as Rosie dropped it in favour of her high-speed camera. She kept darting about ahead of the procession and filming. She had obtained permission for this seemingly disrespectful behaviour from Daisy.

'All historical funerals have photos taken of them,' she had told her. 'It'll make this funeral immortal.'

The others had heard this, and became even more confused by immortality being added to an already inextricable mixture of what was invisible, imaginary and real. The result of this was that hardly anybody among the mourners had any clear conception of what they were supposed to be burying.

They wound their way slowly to Poet's Corner and then halted, still singing, while Daisy got down to business with her trowel. Jack found himself, all at once, understanding what Rosie saw in her. She was so serious – almost dedicated – in whatever she was doing. He cast his eye over the other mourners, almost daring them to giggle. No one as yet showed any signs of doing so, nor were they to do so later.

'There!' Daisy stood up and surveyed her hole with satisfaction. 'You can stop singing now.'

This they obediently and thankfully did.

'This is the funeral of Arry Awk that Arry Awk has come to,' Daisy announced. 'It is a hysterical funeral. There will never be another, not for ever and ever amen.'

She looked about her fellow-mourners for corroboration of this, and they all nodded and assumed appropriate expressions of awe and solemnity.

'There is no need for anybody to cry,' Daisy then told them, 'because Arry Awk i'n't dead. He's here, i'n't you, Arry Awk?' She paused. Then, 'Yes, he is,' she confirmed. 'I will now put him in his coffin. He choosed it himself.'

She picked up the polythene bag and the toffee tin and went through the motions of placing something inside. Her audience all craned forward to see what it was, and for a fleeting moment Jack almost expected to catch a glimpse of Arry Awk himself. He was disappointed. What was actually standing proxy for this invisible person was some kind of blue plastic troll out of a cornflake packet.

Daisy held the tin aloft in her usual manner.

'Oh dear oh dear!' she cried. 'Poor Arry Awk! No more floods and no more eggs! Gone to heaven for ever and ever amen!'

This was all very baffling – and not only in Daisy's confident assignment of her friend to heaven. The Bagthorpes had only a moment ago been instructed that any outward show of grief would be misplaced, yet here was Daisy herself giving every sign of getting into her usual stride, and acting very bereaved indeed. She seemed to have forgotten that Arry Awk was there at her side, witnessing the whole thing. As Jack watched, her face crumpled and tears began to roll down her cheeks.

'Poor little fing!' She was sobbing in earnest now, as she placed the toffee tin into her newly dug hole. 'Oh, dusters to dusters, ashes to ashes! Oh dear, oh dear – Mummy, Mummy, I want him back!'

Aunt Celia, herself weeping, cried:

'No, darling, no! He is not dead, but sleeps!'

'He's dead, he's dead!' wailed Daisy.

Her grief was so real that everyone present began to feel affected – even Grandma, who had always been jealous of Arry Awk's place in Daisy's affections, and would have been only too happy to see him dead.

Daisy was now scattering forlorn little fistfuls of earth on to her tin.

'Oh Arry, Arry,' she sobbed, her face besmirched with soil and tears. 'Don't leave me, Arry! Oh dear – dusters to dusters!'

Uncle Parker, impressed by the way things were going, ventured to put his oar in. He patted his daughter gently on the back.

'Look, Daisy,' he said, 'it's not too late. Fish him out again, why don't you?'

It must have cost him some effort to make this suggestion, because Arry Awk had always been a source of great trouble and expense to him.

'I can't, I can't!' screamed Daisy. 'He's dead! Oh, I wish I never done it! Darling little Arry Awk!'

Grandma, not wishing to appear deficient in feeling, but quite misjudging the depth of Daisy's despair, said:

'It's *always* a shame when somebody dies, Daisy. But you will soon have a new friend – and you have Little Tommy, remember.'

'I don't want Little Tommy,' Daisy screamed passionately, 'I want my Arry Awk back!'

'Don't cry, Daisy,' Jack said. 'Have you forgotten, Arry Awk is *with* you.'

'He i'n't, he i'n't,' she wailed. 'He's just gone down to ashes in that tin!'

The complicated metaphysics of the whole business had evidently become too much for her too, for she no longer seemed to understand it. She had on this occasion, as Mr Bagthorpe later unsympathetically observed, bitten off more than she could chew.

'Anybody who can go around burying people who are dead and alive at the same time has to *expect* to get tied up in knots,' he declared. 'Even Shakespeare never did that, and there's no reason why *she* should expect to get away with it. At least Shakespeare's ghosts were *dead*, for God's sake. Her whole diabolical creation has now ricocheted back on her. It is neither more nor less than poetic justice.'

It was in fact much later on that Mr Bagthorpe made this speech, because at the time when Arry Awk's funeral broke up in disarray, he was occupied in wrestling with a goat, and in no position to utter anything much more than expletives.

How the funeral finally broke up was with Daisy flinging down her floral tribute and fleeing, still sobbing bitterly. Aunt Celia instantly went after her, and the rest of them were left standing there awkwardly, uncertain of what their next move should be.

'Poor old Daisy,' said Jack at last.

'Perhaps it is all for the best,' said Mrs Bagthorpe weakly. (She had never received a Problem relating to Resurrection.)

'D'you think he *is* dead?' asked Rosie nervously. 'Had we better put our flowers on, or not?'

She had gone to some trouble to create a circular wreath, using wire clothes-hangers, beech twigs and roses.

'Better pop 'em on the hole,' Uncle Parker advised. 'Might cheer her up a bit when she sees 'em.'

This they all did, feeling much sadder than they had anticipated. Jack put the bath-salts jar at the head of the grave and propped Daisy's own floral tribute against it. As he did so, he spotted a crumpled piece of Grandma's lavender-scented notepaper. It was Daisy's special epitaph:

> Only me knows Arry Awk
> Only me can here him tawk.

I luv him and he luvs me
And hes as bad as bad can be.
Frinstance won day Arry Awk
Broke sum dums with a nife and fawk.
He had a flood and broke sum eggs
And he mixed up sedes wiv his twinkling legs.
Arry Awks my bestest frend
For evver and evver til the end
Amen.

Jack thought it clear from this composition that Daisy had not in fact contemplated losing Arry Awk in arranging his burial. There was no ring of finality about it – rather the opposite – and, significantly, no date. He himself thought Arry Awk sounded an attractive and lively character from this description, though he supposed that the twinkling legs attributed to him by Daisy were more or less poetic licence, there being few usable rhymes for 'eggs'. He carefully attached this eulogy to the neck of the bath-salts jar and followed the others, all of whom had already left the graveside.

Having been immersed in perusing the epitaph, he had not really noticed all the yelling and screaming up to this juncture, but now he automatically hurried in its direction.

'It really is Hail and Farewell,' he thought.

Three Men in a Boat

JEROME K. JEROME

As a teenager I made the mistake of taking this book to read for the first time on a train. It is very embarrassing to be sitting alone with tears of laughter running down one's face. The book, published in 1889, relates the adventures of three men and a dog, Montmorency, on a boat trip up the Thames. The first extract describes them packing, and the second is an anecdote (and the book is packed with similar ones) about Harris and the Hampton Court Maze.

The food question – Objections to paraffin oil as an atmosphere – Advantages of cheese as a travelling companion – A married woman deserts her home – Further provision for getting upset – I pack – Cussedness of tooth-brushes – George and Harris pack – Awful behaviour of Montmorency – We retire to rest.

★

Then we discussed the food question. George said: 'Begin with breakfast.' (George is so practical.) 'Now for breakfast we shall want a frying-pan' – (Harris said it was indigestible; but we merely urged him not to be an ass, and George went on) – 'a teapot and a kettle, and a methylated spirit stove.'

'No oil,' said George, with a significant look; and Harris and I agreed.

We had taken up an oil-stove once, but 'never again'. It had been like living in an oil-shop that week. It oozed. I never saw such a thing as paraffin oil is to ooze. We kept it in the nose of the boat, and, from there, it oozed down to the rudder, impregnating the whole boat and everything in it on its way, and it oozed over the river, and saturated the scenery and spoilt the atmosphere. Sometimes a westerly oily wind blew, and at other times an easterly oily wind, and sometimes it blew a northerly oily wind, and maybe a southerly oily wind; but whether it came from the Arctic snows, or was raised in the waste of the desert sands, it came alike to us laden with the fragrance of paraffin oil.

And that oil oozed up and ruined the sunset; and as for the moonbeams, they positively reeked of paraffin.

We tried to get away from it at Marlow. We left the boat by the bridge, and took a walk through the town to escape it, but it followed us. The whole town was full of oil. We passed through the churchyard, and it seemed as if the people had been buried in oil.

The High Street stunk of oil; we wondered how people could live in it. And we walked miles upon miles out Birmingham way; but it was no use, the country was steeped in oil.

At the end of that trip we met together at midnight in a lonely field, under a blasted oak, and took an awful oath (we had been swearing for a whole week about the thing in an ordinary, middle-class way, but this was a swell affair) – an awful oath never to take paraffin oil with us in a boat again – except, of course, in case of sickness.

Therefore, in the present instance, we confined ourselves to methylated spirit. Even that is bad enough. You get methylated pie and methylated cake. But methylated spirit is more wholesome when taken into the system in large quantities than paraffin oil.

For other breakfast things, George suggested eggs and bacon which were easy to cook, cold meat, tea, bread and butter, and jam. For lunch, he said, we could have biscuits, cold meat, bread and butter, and jam – but *no cheese*. Cheese, like oil, makes too much of itself. It wants the whole boat to itself. It goes through the hamper, and gives a cheesy flavour to everything else there. You can't tell whether you are eating apple-pie or German sausage, or strawberries and cream. It all seems cheese. There is too much odour about cheese.

I remember a friend of mine buying a couple of cheeses at Liverpool. Splendid cheeses they were, ripe and mellow, and with a two hundred horse-power scent about them that might have been warranted to carry three miles, and knock a man over at two hundred yards. I was in Liverpool at the time, and my friend said that if I didn't mind he would get me to take them back with me to London, as he should not be coming up for a day or two himself, and he did not think the cheeses ought to be kept much longer.

'Oh, with pleasure, dear boy,' I replied, 'with pleasure.'

I called for the cheeses, and took them away in a cab. It was a ramshackle affair, dragged along by a knock-kneed, broken-winded somnambulist, which his owner, in a moment of enthusiasm, during conversation, referred to as a horse. I put the cheeses on the top, and we started off at a shamble that would have done credit to the swiftest steam-roller ever built, and all went merry as a funeral bell, until we turned the corner. There, the wind carried a whiff from the cheeses full on to our steed. It woke him up, and, with a snort of terror, he dashed off at three miles an hour. The wind still blew in his direction, and before we reached the end of the street he was laying himself out at the rate of nearly four miles an hour, leaving the cripples and stout old ladies simply nowhere.

It took two porters as well as the driver to hold him in at the station; and I do not think they would have done it, even then, had not one of the men had the presence of mind to put a handkerchief over his nose, and to light a bit of brown paper.

I took my ticket, and marched proudly up the

platform, with my cheeses, the people falling back respectfully on either side. The train was crowded, and I had to get into a carriage where there were already seven other people. One crusty old gentleman objected, but I got in, notwithstanding; and, putting my cheeses upon the rack, squeezed down with a pleasant smile, and said it was a warm day. A few moments passed, and then the old gentleman began to fidget.

'Very close in here,' he said.

'Quite oppressive,' said the man next him.

And then they both began sniffing, and, at the third sniff, they caught it right on the chest, and rose up without another word and went out. And then a stout lady got up, and said it was disgraceful that a respectable married woman should be harried about in this way, and gathered up a bag and eight parcels and went. The remaining four passengers sat on for a while, until a solemn-looking man in the corner who, from his dress and general appearance, seemed to belong to the undertaker class, said it put him in mind of a dead baby; and the other three passengers tried to get out of the door at the same time, and hurt themselves.

I smiled at the black gentleman, and said I thought we were going to have the carriage to ourselves; and he laughed pleasantly and said that some people made such a fuss over a little thing. But even he grew strangely depressed after we had started, and so, when we reached Crewe, I asked him to come and have a

drink. He accepted, and we forced our way into the
buffet, where we yelled, and stamped, and waved our
umbrellas for a quarter of an hour; and then a young
lady came and asked us if we wanted anything.

'What's yours?' I said, turning to my friend.

'I'll have half-a-crown's worth of brandy, neat, if
you please, miss,' he responded.

And he went off quickly after he had drunk it and
got into another carriage, which I thought mean.

From Crewe I had the compartment to myself,
though the train was crowded. As we drew up at the
different stations, the people, seeing my empty carriage, would rush for it. 'Here y' are, Maria; come
along, plenty of room.' 'All right, Tom; we'll get in
here,' they would shout. And they would run along,
carrying heavy bags, and fight round the door to get
in first. And one would open the door and mount the
steps and stagger back into the arms of the man behind
him; and they would all come and have a sniff, and
then droop off and squeeze into other carriages, or
pay the difference and go first.

From Euston I took the cheese down to my friend's
house. When his wife came into the room she smelt
round for an instant. Then she said:

'What is it? Tell me the worst.'

I said:

'It's cheeses. Tom bought them in Liverpool, and
asked me to bring them up with me.'

And I added that I hoped she understood that it had
nothing to do with me; and she said that she was sure of

that, but that she would speak to Tom about it when he came back.

My friend was detained in Liverpool longer than he expected; and three days later, as he hadn't returned home, his wife called on me. She said:

'What did Tom say about those cheeses?'

I replied that he had directed they were to be kept in a moist place, and that nobody was to touch them.

She said:

'Nobody's likely to touch them. Had he smelt them?'

I thought he had, and added that he seemed greatly attached to them.

'You think he would be upset,' she queried, 'if I gave a man a sovereign to take them away and bury them?'

I answered that I thought he would never smile again.

An idea struck her. She said:

'Do you mind keeping them for him? Let me send them round to you.'

'Madam,' I replied, 'for myself I like the smell of cheese, and the journey the other day with them from Liverpool I shall ever look back upon as a happy ending to a pleasant holiday. But, in this world, we must consider others. The lady under whose roof I have the honour of residing is a widow, and, for all I know, possibly an orphan too. She has a strong, I may say an eloquent, objection to being what she terms "put upon." The presence of your husband's cheeses in her house she would, I instinctively feel, regard as a "put upon"; and it shall never be said that I put upon the widow and the orphan.'

'Very well, then,' said my friend's wife, rising, 'all I have to say is, that I shall take the children and go to an hotel until those cheeses are eaten. I decline to live any longer in the same house with them.'

She kept her word, leaving the place in charge of the char-woman, who, when asked if she could stand the smell, replied, 'What smell?' and who, when taken close to the cheeses and told to sniff hard, said she could detect a faint odour of melons. It was argued from this that little injury could result to the woman from the atmosphere, and she was left.

The hotel bill came to fifteen guineas; and my friend, after reckoning everything up, found that the cheeses had cost him eight-and-sixpence a pound. He said he dearly loved a bit of cheese, but it was beyond his means; so he determined to get rid of them. He threw them into the canal; but had to fish them out again, as the bargemen complained. They said it made them feel quite faint. And, after that, he took them one dark night and left them in the parish mortuary. But the coroner discovered them, and made a fearful fuss.

He said it was a plot to deprive him of his living by waking up the corpses.

My friend got rid of them, at last, by taking them down to a seaside town, and burying them on the beach. It gained the place quite a reputation. Visitors said they had never noticed before how strong the air was, and weak-chested and consumptive people used to throng there for years afterwards.

Fond as I am of cheese, therefore, I hold that George was right in declining to take any.

'We shan't want any tea,' said George (Harris's face fell at this); 'but we'll have a good round, square, slap-up meal at seven – dinner, tea, and supper combined.'

Harris grew more cheerful. George suggested meat and fruit pies, cold meat, tomatoes, fruit, and green stuff. For drink, we took some wonderful sticky concoction of Harris's, which you mixed with water and called lemonade, plenty of tea, and a bottle of whisky, in case, as George said, we got upset.

It seemed to me that George harped too much on the getting-upset idea. It seemed to me the wrong spirit to go about the trip in.

But I'm glad we took the whisky.

We didn't take beer or wine. They are a mistake up the river. They make you feel sleepy and heavy. A glass in the evening when you are doing a mooch round the town and looking at the girls is all right enough; but don't drink when the sun is blazing down on your head, and you've got hard work to do.

We made a list of the things to be taken, and a pretty lengthy one it was before we parted that evening. The next day, which was Friday, we got them all together, and met in the evening to pack. We got a big Gladstone for the clothes, and a couple of hampers for the victuals and the cooking utensils. We moved the table up against the window, piled everything in a heap in the middle of the floor, and sat round and looked at it.

I said I'd pack.

I rather pride myself on my packing. Packing is one of those many things that I feel I know more about than any other person living. (It surprises me myself, sometimes, how many of these subjects there are.) I impressed the fact upon George and Harris and told them that they had better leave the whole matter entirely to me. They fell into the suggestion with a readiness that had something uncanny about it. George put on a pipe and spread himself over the easy-chair, and Harris cocked his legs on the table and lit a cigar.

This was hardly what I intended. What I had meant, of course, was, that I should boss the job, and that Harris and George should potter about under my directions, I pushing them aside every now and then with, 'Oh, you —!' 'Here, let me do it.' 'There you are, simple enough!' – really teaching them, as you might say. Their taking it in the way they did irritated me. There is nothing does irritate me more than seeing other people sitting about doing nothing when I'm working.

I lived with a man once who used to make me mad that way. He would loll on the sofa and watch me doing things by the hour together, following me round the room with his eyes, wherever I went. He said it made him feel that life was not an idle dream to be gaped and yawned through, but a noble task, full of duty and stern work. He said he often wondered now how he could have gone on before he met me, never having anybody to look at while they worked.

Now, I'm not like that. I can't sit still and see another man slaving and working. I want to get up and superintend, and walk round with my hands in my pockets, and tell him what to do. It is my energetic nature. I can't help it.

However, I did not say anything, but started the packing. It seemed a longer job than I had thought it was going to be; but I got the bag finished at last, and I sat on it and strapped it.

'Ain't you going to put the boots in?' said Harris.

And I looked round, and found I had forgotten them. That's just like Harris. He couldn't have said a word until I'd got the bag shut and strapped, of course. And George laughed – one of those irritating, sense-less, chuckle-headed, crack-jawed laughs of his. They do make me so wild.

I opened the bag and packed the boots in; and then, just as I was going to close it, a horrible idea occurred to me. Had I packed my tooth-brush? I don't know how it is, but I never do know whether I've packed my tooth-brush.

My tooth-brush is a thing that haunts me when I'm travelling, and makes my life a misery. I dream that I haven't packed it, and wake up in a cold perspiration, and get out of bed and hunt for it. And, in the morn-ing, I pack it before I have used it, and have to unpack again to get it, and it is always the last thing I turn out of the bag; and then I repack and forget it, and have to rush upstairs for it at the last moment and carry it to the railway station, wrapped up in my pocket-handkerchief.

Of course I had to turn every mortal thing out now, and, of course, I could not find it. I rummaged the things up into much the same state that they must have been before the world was created, and when chaos reigned. Of course, I found George's and Harris's eighteen times over, but I couldn't find my own. I put the things back one by one, and held everything up and shook it. Then I found it inside a boot. I repacked once more.

When I had finished, George asked if the soap was in. I said I didn't care a hang whether the soap was in or whether it wasn't; and I slammed the bag to and strapped it, and found that I had packed my tobacco-pouch in it, and had to re-open it. It got shut up finally at 10.5 p.m., and then there remained the hampers to do. Harris said that we should be wanting to start in less than twelve hours' time and thought that he and George had better do the rest; and I agreed and sat down, and they had a go.

They began in a light-hearted spirit, evidently intending to show me how to do it. I made no comment; I only waited. When George is hanged Harris will be the worst packer in this world; and I looked at the piles of plates and cups, and kettles, and bottles, and jars, and pies, and stoves, and cakes, and tomatoes, etc., and felt that the thing would soon become exciting.

It did. They started with breaking a cup. That was the first thing they did. They did that just to show you what they *could* do, and to get you interested.

Then Harris packed the strawberry jam on top of a tomato and squashed it, and they had to pick out the tomato with a teaspoon.

And then it was George's turn, and he trod on the butter. I didn't say anything, but I came over and sat on the edge of the table and watched them. It irritated them more than anything I could have said. I felt that. It made them nervous and excited, and they stepped on things, and put things behind them, and then couldn't find them when they wanted them; and they packed the pies at the bottom, and put heavy things on top, and smashed the pies in.

They upset salt over everything, and as for the butter! I never saw two men do more with one-and-twopence worth of butter in my whole life than they did. After George had got it off his slipper, they tried to put it in the kettle. It wouldn't go in, and what *was* in wouldn't come out. They did scrape it out at last, and put it down on a chair, and Harris sat on it, and it stuck to him, and they went looking for it all over the room.

'I'll take my oath I put it down on that chair,' said George, staring at the empty seat.

'I saw you do it myself, not a minute ago,' said Harris.

Then they started round the room again looking for it; and then they met again in the centre and stared at one another.

'Most extraordinary thing I ever heard of,' said George.

'So mysterious!' said Harris.

Then George got round at the back of Harris and saw it.

'Why, here it is all the time,' he exclaimed, indignantly.

'Where?' cried Harris, spinning round.

'Stand still, can't you!' roared George, flying after him.

And they got it off, and packed it in the teapot.

Montmorency was in it all, of course. Montmorency's ambition in life, is to get in the way and be sworn at. If he can squirm in anywhere where he particularly is not wanted, and be a perfect nuisance, and make people mad, and have things thrown at his head, then he feels his day has not been wasted.

To get somebody to stumble over him, and curse him steadily for an hour, is his highest aim and object; and, when he has succeeded in accomplishing this, his conceit becomes quite unbearable.

He came and sat down on things, just when they were wanted to be packed; and he laboured under the fixed belief that, whenever Harris or George reached out their hand for anything, it was his cold damp nose that they wanted. He put his leg into the jam, and he worried the teaspoons, and he pretended that the lemons were rats, and got into the hamper and killed three of them before Harris could land him with the frying-pan.

Harris said I encouraged him. I didn't encourage him. A dog like that don't want any encouragement. It's the natural, original sin that is born in him that makes him do things like that.

The packing was done at 12.50; and Harris sat on the big hamper, and said he hoped nothing would be found broken. George said that if anything was broken it *was* broken, which reflection seemed to comfort him. He also said he was ready for bed. We were all ready for bed. Harris was to sleep with us that night, and we went upstairs.

We tossed for beds, and Harris had to sleep with me. He said:

'Do you prefer the inside or the outside, J.?'

I said I generally preferred to sleep *inside* a bed.

Harris said it was old.

George said:

'What time shall I wake you fellows?'

Harris said:

'Seven.'

I said:

'No – six,' because I wanted to write some letters.

Harris and I had a bit of a row over it, but at last split the difference, and said half-past six.

'Wake us at 6.30, George,' we said.

George made no answer, and we found, on going over, that he had been asleep for some time; so we placed the bath where he could tumble into it on getting out in the morning, and went to bed ourselves.

Harris asked me if I'd ever been in the maze at Hampton Court. He said he went in once to show somebody else the way. He had studied it up in a map, and it was so simple that it seemed foolish – hardly worth the twopence charged for admission. Harris said he thought that map must have been got up as a practical joke, because it wasn't a bit like the real thing, and only misleading. It was a country cousin that Harris took in. He said:

'We'll just go in here, so that you can say you've been, but it's very simple. It's absurd to call it a maze. You keep on taking the first turning to the right. We'll just walk round for ten minutes, and then go and get some lunch.'

They met some people soon after they had got inside, who said they had been there for threequarters of an hour, and had had about enough of it. Harris told them they could follow him if they liked; he was just going in, and then should turn round and come out again. They said it was very kind of him, and fell behind, and followed.

They picked up various other people who wanted to get it over, as they went along, until they had absorbed all the persons in the maze. People who had given up all hopes of ever getting either in or out, or of ever seeing their home and friends again, plucked up courage, at the sight of Harris and his party, and joined the procession, blessing him. Harris said he should judge there must have been twenty people following him, in all; and one woman with a baby, who had been there all the morning, insisted on taking his arm, for fear of losing him.

Harris kept on turning to the right, but it seemed a long way, and his cousin said he supposed it was a very big maze.

'Oh, one of the largest in Europe,' said Harris.

'Yes, it must be,' replied the cousin, 'because we've walked a good two miles already.'

Harris began to think it rather strange himself, but he held on until, at last, they passed the half of a penny bun on the ground that Harris's cousin swore he had noticed there seven minutes ago. Harris said: 'Oh, impossible!' but the woman with the baby said, 'Not at all,' as she herself had taken it from the child, and thrown it down there, just before she met Harris. She also added that she wished she never had met Harris, and expressed an opinion that he was an impostor. That made Harris mad, and he produced his map, and explained his theory.

'The map may be all right enough,' said one of the party, 'if you know whereabouts in it we are now.'

Harris didn't know, and suggested that the best thing to do would be to go back to the entrance, and begin again. For the beginning again part of it there was not much enthusiasm; but with regard to the advisability of going back to the entrance there was complete unanimity, and so they turned, and trailed after Harris again, in the opposite direction. About ten minutes more passed, and then they found themselves in the centre.

Harris thought at first of pretending that that was what he had been aiming at; but the crowd looked dangerous, and he decided to treat it as an accident.

Anyhow, they had got something to start from then. They did know where they were, and the map was once more consulted, and the thing seemed simpler than ever, and off they started for the third time.

And three minutes later they were back in the centre again.

After that they simply couldn't get anywhere else. Whatever way they turned brought them back to the middle. It became so regular at length, that some of the people stopped there, and waited for the others to take a walk round, and come back to them. Harris drew out his map again, after a while, but the sight of it only infuriated the mob, and they told him to go and curl his hair with it. Harris said that he couldn't help feeling that, to a certain extent, he had become unpopular.

They all got crazy at last, and sang out for the keeper, and the man came and climbed up the ladder outside, and shouted out directions to them. But all their heads were, by this time, in such a confused whirl that they were incapable of grasping anything, and so the man told them to stop where they were, and he would come to them. They huddled together, and waited; and he climbed down, and came in.

He was a young keeper, as luck would have it, and new to the business; and when he got in, he couldn't get to them, and then *he* got lost. They caught sight of him, every now and then, rushing about the other side of the hedge, and he would see them, and rush to get to them, and they would wait there for about five minutes, and then he would reappear again in exactly the same spot, and ask them where they had been.

They had to wait until one of the old keepers came back from his dinner before they got out.

Harris said he thought it was a very fine maze, so far as he was a judge; and we agreed that we would try to get George to go into it, on our way back.

The Secret Diary of Adrian Mole Aged 13¾

SUE TOWNSEND

This book is a phenomenon of modern publishing. Its appeal is to both children and adults. It first appeared in 1982 and my guess is it will never be out of print. It has also been made into a successful television series.

Thursday   January 1st

BANK HOLIDAY IN ENGLAND,
IRELAND, SCOTLAND AND WALES

These are my New Year's resolutions:

1. I will help the blind across the road.
2. I will hang my trousers up.
3. I will put the sleeves back on my records.
4. I will not start smoking.
5. I will stop squeezing my spots.

6. I will be kind to the dog.
7. I will help the poor and ignorant.
8. After hearing the disgusting noises from downstairs last night, I have also vowed never to drink alcohol.

My father got the dog drunk on cherry brandy at the party last night. If the RSPCA hear about it he could get done. Eight days have gone by since Christmas Day but my mother still hasn't worn the green lurex apron I bought her for Christmas! She will get bathcubes next year.

Just my luck, I've got a spot on my chin for the first day of the New Year!

Friday   January 2nd

BANK HOLIDAY IN SCOTLAND. FULL MOON

I felt rotten today. It's my mother's fault for singing 'My Way' at two o'clock in the morning at the top of the stairs. Just my luck to have a mother like her. There is a chance my parents could be alcoholics. Next year I could be in a children's home.

The dog got its own back on my father. It jumped up and knocked down his model ship, then ran into the garden with the rigging tangled in its feet. My father kept saying, 'Three months' work down the drain', over and over again.

The spot on my chin is getting bigger. It's my mother's fault for not knowing about vitamins.

Saturday   January 3rd

I shall go mad through lack of sleep! My father has banned the dog from the house so it barked outside my window all night. Just my luck! My father shouted a swear-word at it. If he's not careful he will get done by the police for obscene language.

I think the spot is a boil. Just my luck to have it where everybody can see it. I pointed out to my mother that I hadn't had any vitamin C today. She said, 'Go and buy an orange, then'. This is typical.

She still hasn't worn the lurex apron.

I will be glad to get back to school.

Sunday   January 4th

SECOND AFTER CHRISTMAS

My father has got the flu. I'm not surprised with the diet we get. My mother went out in the rain to get him a vitamin C drink, but as I told her, 'It's too late now'. It's a miracle we don't get scurvy. My mother says she can't see anything on my chin, but this is guilt because of the diet.

The dog has run off because my mother didn't close the gate. I have broken the arm on the stereo. Nobody knows yet, and with a bit of luck my father will be ill for a long time. He is the only one who uses it apart from me. No sign of the apron.

Monday   January 5th

The dog hasn't come back yet. It is peaceful without it. My mother rang the police and gave a description of the dog. She made it sound worse than it actually is: straggly hair over its eyes and all that. I really think the police have got better things to do than look for dogs, such as catching murderers. I told my mother this but she still rang them. Serve her right if she was murdered because of the dog.

My father is still lazing about in bed. He is supposed to be ill, but I noticed he is still smoking!

Nigel came round today. He has got a tan from his Christmas holiday. I think Nigel will be ill soon from the shock of the cold in England. I think Nigel's parents were wrong to take him abroad.

He hasn't got a single spot yet.

Tuesday   January 6th

EPIPHANY. NEW MOON

The dog is in trouble!

It knocked a meter-reader off his bike and messed all the cards up. So now we will all end up in court I expect. A policeman said we must keep the dog under control and asked how long it had been lame. My mother said it wasn't lame, and examined it. There was a tiny model pirate trapped in its left front paw.

The dog was pleased when my mother took the

pirate out and it jumped up the policeman's tunic with its muddy paws. My mother fetched a cloth from the kitchen but it had strawberry jam on it where I had wiped the knife, so the tunic was worse than ever. The policeman went then. I'm sure he swore. I could report him for that.

I will look up 'Epiphany' in my new dictionary.

Wednesday   January 7th

Nigel came round on his new bike this morning. It has got a water bottle, a milometer, a speedometer, a yellow saddle, and very thin racing wheels. It's wasted on Nigel. He only goes to the shops and back on it. If I had it, I would go all over the country and have an experience.

My spot or boil has reached its peak. Surely it can't get any bigger!

I found a word in my dictionary that describes my father. It is *malingerer*. He is still in bed guzzling vitamin C.

The dog is locked in the coal shed.

Epiphany is something to do with the three wise men. Big deal!

Thursday   January 8th

Now my mother has got the flu. This means that I have to look after them both. Just my luck!

I have been up and down the stairs all day. I cooked a big dinner for them tonight: two poached eggs with beans, and tinned semolina pudding. (It's a good job I wore the green lurex apron because the poached eggs escaped out of the pan and got all over me.) I nearly said something when I saw they hadn't eaten *any* of it. They can't be that ill. I gave it to the dog in the coal shed. My grandmother is coming tomorrow morning, so I had to clean the burnt saucepans, then take the dog for a walk. It was half past eleven before I got to bed. No wonder I am short for my age.

I have decided against medicine for a career.

Friday   January 9th

It was cough, cough, cough last night. If it wasn't one it was the other. You'd think they'd show some consideration after the hard day I'd had.

My grandma came and was disgusted with the state of the house. I showed her my room which is always neat and tidy and she gave me fifty pence. I showed her all the empty drink bottles in the dustbin and she was disgusted.

My grandma let the dog out of the coal shed. She said my mother was cruel to lock it up. The dog was sick on the kitchen floor. My grandma locked it up again.

She squeezed the spot on my chin. It has made it worse. I told grandma about the green apron and grandma said that she bought my mother a one hundred per cent acrylic cardigan every Christmas and my mother had *never ever* worn one of them!

Saturday January 10th

a.m. Now the dog is ill! It keeps being sick so the vet has got to come. My father told me not to tell the vet that the dog had been locked in the coal shed for two days.

I have put a plaster over the spot to stop germs getting in it from the dog.

The vet has taken the dog away. He says he thinks it has got an obstruction and will need an emergency operation.

My grandma has had a row with my mother and gone home. My grandma found the Christmas cardigans all cut up in the duster bag. It is disgusting when people are starving.

Mr Lucas from next door has been in to see my mother and father who are still in bed. He brought a 'get well' card and some flowers for my mother. My mother sat up in bed in a nightie that showed a lot of her chest. She talked to Mr Lucas in a yukky voice. My father pretended to be asleep.

Nigel brought his records round. He is into punk, but I don't see the point if you can't hear the words. Anyway I think I'm turning into an intellectual. It must be all the worry.

p.m. I went to see how the dog is. It has had its operation. The vet showed me a plastic bag with lots of yukky things in it. There was a lump of coal, the fir tree from the Christmas cake, and the model pirates from my father's ship. One of the pirates was waving a cutlass which must have been very painful for the dog. The dog looks a lot better. It can come home in two days, worse luck.

My father was having a row with my grandma on the phone about the empty bottles in the dustbin when I got home.

Mr Lucas was upstairs talking to my mother. When Mr Lucas went, my father went upstairs and had an argument with my mother and made her cry. My father is in a bad mood. This means he is feeling better. I made my mother a cup of tea without her asking. This made her cry as well. You can't please some people!

The spot is still there.

Sunday   January 11th

FIRST AFTER EPIPHANY

Now I *know* I am an intellectual. I saw Malcolm Muggeridge on the television last night, and I understood nearly every word. It all adds up. A bad home, poor diet, not liking punk. I think I will join the library and see what happens.

It is a pity there aren't any more intellectuals living

round here. Mr Lucas wears corduroy trousers, but he's an insurance man. Just my luck.

The first what after Epiphany?

Monday January 12th

The dog is back. It keeps licking its stitches, so when I am eating I sit with my back to it.

My mother got up this morning to make the dog a bed to sleep in until it's better. It is made out of a cardboard box that used to contain packets of soap powder. My father said this would make the dog sneeze and burst its stitches, and the vet would charge even more to stitch it back up again. They had a row about the box, then my father went on about Mr Lucas. Though what Mr Lucas has to do with the dog's bed is a mystery to me.

Tuesday January 13th

My father has gone back to work. Thank God! I don't know how my mother sticks him.

Mr Lucas came in this morning to see if my mother needed any help in the house. He is very kind. Mrs Lucas was next door cleaning the outside windows. The ladder didn't look very safe. I have written to Malcolm Muggeridge, c/o the BBC, asking him what to do about being an intellectual. I hope he writes back soon because I'm getting fed up being one on my own. I have written a poem, and it only took me two minutes. Even the famous poets take longer than that. It is called 'The Tap', but it isn't really about a tap, it's very deep, and about life and stuff like that.

> *The Tap, by Adrian Mole*
> The tap drips and keeps me awake,
> In the morning there will be a lake.
> For the want of a washer the carpet will spoil,
> Then for another my father will toil.
> My father could snuff it while he is at work.
> Dad, fit a washer don't be a burk!

I showed it to my mother, but she laughed. She isn't very bright. She still hasn't washed my PE shorts, and it is school tomorrow. She is not like the mothers on television.

Wednesday   January 14th

Joined the library. Got *Care of the Skin*, *Origin of Species*, and a book by a woman my mother is always going on about. It is called *Pride and Prejudice*, by a woman called Jane Austen. I could tell the librarian was impressed. Perhaps she is an intellectual like me. She didn't look at my spot, so perhaps it is getting smaller. About time!

Mr Lucas was in the kitchen drinking coffee with

my mother. The room was full of smoke. They were laughing, but when I went in, they stopped.

Mrs Lucas was next door cleaning the drains. She looked as if she was in a bad mood. I think Mr and Mrs Lucas have got an unhappy marriage. Poor Mr Lucas!

None of the teachers at school have noticed that I am an intellectual. They will be sorry when I am famous. There is a new girl in our class. She sits next to me in Geography. She is all right. Her name is Pandora, but she likes being called 'Box'. Don't ask me why. I might fall in love with her. It's time I fell in love, after all I am 13¾ years old.

Thursday January 15th

Pandora has got hair the colour of treacle, and it's long like girls' hair should be. She has got quite a good figure. I saw her playing netball and her chest was wobbling. I felt a bit funny. I think this is it!

The dog has had its stitches out. It bit the vet, but I expect he's used to it. (The vet I mean; I know the dog is.)

My father found out about the arm on the stereo. I told a lie. I said the dog jumped up and broke it. My father said he will wait until the dog is completely cured of its operation then kick it. I hope this is a joke.

Mr Lucas was in the kitchen again when I got

home from school. My mother is better now, so why he keeps coming round is a mystery to me. Mrs Lucas was planting trees in the dark. I read a bit of *Pride and Prejudice*, but it was very old-fashioned. I think Jane Austen should write something a bit more modern.

The dog has got the same colour eyes as Pandora. I only noticed because my mother cut the dog's hair. It looks worse than ever. Mr Lucas and my mother were laughing at the dog's new haircut which is not very nice, because dogs can't answer back, just like the Royal Family.

I am going to bed early to think about Pandora and do my back-stretching exercises. I haven't grown for two weeks. If this carries on I will be a midget.

I will go to the doctor's on Saturday if the spot is still there. I can't live like this with everybody staring.

Friday   January 16th

Mr Lucas came round and offered to take my mother shopping in the car. They dropped me off at school. I was glad to get out of the car what with all the laughing and cigarette smoke. We saw Mrs Lucas on the way. She was carrying big bags of shopping. My mother waved, but Mrs Lucas couldn't wave back.

It was Geography today so I sat next to Pandora for a whole hour. She looks better every day. I told her about her eyes being the same as the dog's. She asked what kind of dog it was. I told her it was a mongrel.

I lent Pandora my blue felt-tip pen to colour round the British Isles.

I think she appreciates these small attentions.

I started *Origin of Species* today, but it's not as good as the television series. *Care of the Skin* is dead good. I have left it open on the pages about vitamins. I hope my mother takes the hint. I have left it on the kitchen table near the ashtray, so she is bound to see it.

I have made an appointment about the spot. It has turned purple.

Saturday   January 17th

I was woken up early this morning. Mrs Lucas is concreting the front of their house, and the concrete lorry had to keep its engine running while she shovelled the concrete round before it set. Mr Lucas made her a cup of tea. He really is kind.

Nigel came round to see if I wanted to go to the pictures but I told him I couldn't, because I was going to the doctor's about the spot. He said he couldn't see a spot, but he was just being polite because the spot is massive today.

Dr Taylor must be one of those overworked GPs you are always reading about. He didn't examine the spot, he just said I mustn't worry and was everything all right at home. I told him about my bad home life and my poor diet, but he said I was well nourished and to go home and count my blessings. So much for the National Health Service.

I will get a paper-round and go private.

Sunday   January 18th

SECOND AFTER EPIPHANY.

OXFORD HILARY TERM STARTS

Mrs Lucas and my mother have had a row over the dog. Somehow it escaped from the house and trampled on Mrs Lucas's wet concrete. My father offered to have the dog put down, but my mother started to cry so he said he wouldn't. All the neighbours were out in the street washing their cars and listening. Sometimes I really hate the dog!

I remembered my resolution about helping the poor and ignorant today, so I took some of my old *Beano* annuals to a quite poor family who have moved into the next street. I know they are poor because they have only got a black and white telly. A boy answered the door. I explained why I had come. He looked at the annuals and said, 'I've read 'em', and slammed the door in my face. So much for helping the poor!

Monday   January 19th

I have joined a group at school called the Good Samaritans. We go out into the community helping and stuff like that. We miss Maths on Monday afternoons.

Today we had a talk on the sort of things we will be doing. I have been put in the old age pensioners' group. Nigel has got a dead yukky job looking after kids in a playgroup. He is as sick as a parrot.

I can't wait for next Monday. I will get a cassette so I can tape all the old fogies' stories about the war and stuff. I hope I get one with a good memory.

The dog is back at the vet's. It has got concrete stuck on its paws. No wonder it was making such a row on the stairs last night. Pandora smiled at me in school dinner today, but I was choking on a piece of gristle so I couldn't smile back. Just my luck!

Tuesday January 20th

FULL MOON

My mother is looking for a job!

Now I could end up a delinquent roaming the streets and all that. And what will I do during the holidays? I expect I will have to sit in a launderette all day to keep warm. I will be a latchkey kid, whatever that is. And who will look after the dog? And what will I have to eat all day? I will be forced to eat crisps and sweets until my skin is ruined and my teeth fall out. I think my mother is being very selfish. She won't be any good in a job anyway. She isn't very bright and she drinks too much at Christmas.

I rang my grandma up and told her, and she says I could stay at her house in the holidays, and go to the Evergreens' meetings in the afternoons and stuff like that. I wish I hadn't rung now. The Samaritans met today during break. The old people were shared out. I got an old man called Bert Baxter. He is eighty-nine so I don't suppose I'll have him for long. I'm going round to see him tomorrow. I hope he hasn't got a dog. I'm fed up with dogs. They are either at the vet's or standing in front of the television.

Wednesday   January 21st

Mr and Mrs Lucas are getting a divorce! They are the first down our road. My mother went next door to comfort Mr Lucas. He must have been very upset because she was still there when my father came home from work. Mrs Lucas has gone somewhere in a taxi. I think she has left for ever because she has taken her socket set with her. Poor Mr Lucas, now he will have to do his own washing and stuff.

My father cooked the tea tonight. We had boil-in-the-bag curry and rice, it was the only thing left in the freezer apart from a bag of green stuff which has lost its label. My father made a joke about sending it to the public health inspector. My mother didn't laugh. Perhaps she was thinking about poor Mr Lucas left on his own.

I went to see old Mr Baxter after tea. My father

dropped me off on his way to play badminton. Mr Baxter's house is hard to see from the road. It has got a massive overgrown privet hedge all round it. When I knocked on the door a dog started barking and growling and jumping up at the letterbox. I heard the sound of bottles being knocked over and a man swearing before I ran off. I hope I have got the wrong number.

I saw Nigel on the way home. He told me Pandora's father is a milkman! I have gone off her a bit.

Nobody was in when I got home so I fed the dog, looked at my spots and went to bed.

Thursday   January 22nd

It is a dirty lie about Pandora's father being a milkman! He is an accountant at the dairy. Pandora says she will duff Nigel up if he goes round committing libel. I am in love with her again.

Nigel has asked me to go to a disco at the youth club tomorrow night; it is being held to raise funds for a new packet of ping-pong balls. I don't know if I will go because Nigel is a punk at weekends. His mother lets him be one providing he wears a string vest under his bondage T-shirt.

My mother has got an interview for a job. She is practising her typing and not doing any cooking. So what will it be like if she *gets* the job? My father should put his foot down before we are a broken home.

Friday   January 23rd

That is the last time I go to a disco. Everybody there was a punk except me and Rick Lemon, the youth leader. Nigel was showing off all night. He ended up putting a safety pin through his ear. My father had to take him to the hospital in our car. Nigel's parents haven't got a car because his father's got a steel plate in his head and his mother is only four feet eleven inches tall. It's not surprising Nigel has turned out bad really, with a maniac and a midget for parents.

I still haven't heard from Malcolm Muggeridge. Perhaps he is in a bad mood. Intellectuals like him and me often have bad moods. Ordinary people don't understand us and say we are sulking, but we're not.

Pandora has been to see Nigel in hospital. He has got a bit of blood poisoning from the safety pin. Pandora thinks Nigel is dead brave. I think he is dead stupid.

I have had a headache all day because of my mother's rotten typing, but I'm not complaining. I must go to sleep now. I've got to go and see Bert Baxter tomorrow at his house. It was the right number **WORSE LUCK!**

Saturday   January 24th

Today was the most terrible day of my life. My mother has got a job doing her rotten typing in an insurance office! She starts on Monday! Mr Lucas works at the same place. He is going to give her a lift every day.

And my father is in a bad mood – he thinks his big-end is going.

But worst of all, Bert Baxter is not a nice old age pensioner! He drinks and smokes and has an Alsatian dog called Sabre. Sabre was locked in the kitchen while I was cutting the massive hedge, but he didn't stop growling once.

But even worse than that! Pandora is going out with Nigel!!!!! I think I will never get over this shock.

Sunday   January 25th

THIRD AFTER EPIPHANY
10 a.m. I am ill with all the worry, too weak to write much. Nobody has noticed I haven't eaten any breakfast.
2 p.m. Had two junior aspirins at midday and rallied a bit. Perhaps when I am famous and my diary is discovered people will understand the torment of being a 13¾-year-old undiscovered intellectual.
6 p.m. Pandora! My lost love!

Now I will never stroke your treacle hair! (Although my blue felt-tip is still at your disposal.)

8 p.m. Pandora! Pandora! Pandora!
10 p.m. Why? Why? Why?
Midnight. Had a crab-paste sandwich and a satsuma (for the good of my skin). Feel a bit better. I hope Nigel falls off his bike and is squashed flat by a lorry. I will never speak to him again. He knew I was in love with Pandora! If I'd had a racing-bike for Christmas instead of a lousy digital stereo alarm clock, none of this would have happened.

Monday   January 26th

I had to leave my sick-bed to visit Bert Baxter before school. It took me ages to get there, what with feeling weak and having to stop for a rest every now and again, but with the help of an old lady who had a long black moustache I made it to the front door. Bert Baxter was in bed but he threw the key down and I let myself in. Sabre was locked in the bathroom; he was growling and sounded as if he was ripping up towels or something.

Bert Baxter was lying in a filthy-looking bed smoking a cigarette, there was a horrible smell in the room, I think it came from Bert Baxter himself. The bed sheets looked as though they were covered in blood, but Bert said that was caused by the beetroot sandwiches he always eats last thing at night. It was the most disgusting room I have ever seen (and I'm no stranger to squalor). Bert Baxter gave me ten pence and asked me to get him the *Morning Star* from the newsagent's. So he is a communist as well as everything else! Sabre usually fetches the paper but he is being kept in as a punishment for chewing the sink.

The man in the newsagent's asked me to give Bert Baxter his bill (he owes for his papers, £31.97), but when I did Bert Baxter said, 'Smarmy four-eyed git', and laughed and ripped the bill up. I was late for school so I had to go to the school secretary's office and have my name put in the late book. That's the gratitude I get for being a Good Samaritan! I didn't miss Maths either! Saw Pandora and Nigel standing close together in the dinner queue but chose to ignore them.

Mr Lucas has taken to his bed because of being deserted so my mother is taking care of him when she finishes work. She is the only person he will see. So when will she find time to look after me and my father?

My father is sulking, I think he must be jealous because Mr Lucas doesn't want to see *him*.

Midnight. Goodnight Pandora my treacle-haired love.

XXXXXXXXX

Tuesday   January 27th

Art was dead good today. I painted a lonely boy standing on a bridge. The boy had just lost his first love to his ex-best friend. The ex-best friend was struggling in the torrential river. The boy was watching his ex-best friend drown. The ex-best friend looked a bit like Nigel. The boy looked a bit like me. Ms Fossington-Gore said my picture 'had depth', so did the river. Ha! Ha! Ha!

Wednesday January 28th

LAST QUARTER

I woke up with a bit of a cold this morning. I asked my mother for a note to excuse me from games. She said she refused to namby-pamby me a day longer! How would she like to run about on a muddy field in the freezing drizzle, dressed only in PE shorts and a singlet? When I was in the school sports day three-legged race last year she came to watch me, *and* she had her fur coat on *and* she put a blanket round her legs, *and* it was only June! Anyway my mother is sorry now, we had rugger and my PE stuff was so full of mud that it has clogged up the drain hose on the washing-machine.

The vet rang up to demand that we come and fetch the dog back from his surgery. It has been there nine days. My father says it will have to stay there until he gets paid tomorrow. The vet only takes cash and my father hasn't got any.

Pandora! Why?

Thursday January 29th

The stupid dog is back. I am not taking it for a walk until its hair grows back on its shaved paws. My father looked pale when he came home from the vet's, he kept saying 'It's money down the drain', and he said that from now on the dog can only be fed on leftovers from his plate.

This means the dog will soon starve.

Friday January 30th

That filthy commie Bert Baxter has phoned the school to complain that I left the hedge-clippers out in the rain! He claims that they have gone all rusty. He wants compensation. I told Mr Scruton, the headmaster, that they were already rusty but I could tell he didn't believe me. He gave me a lecture on how hard it was for old people to make ends meet. He has ordered me to go to Bert Baxter's and clean and sharpen the hedge-clippers. I wanted to tell the headmaster all about horrible Bert Baxter but there is something about Mr Scruton that makes my mind go blank. I think it's the way his eyes pop out when he is in a temper.

On the way to Bert Baxter's I saw my mother and Mr Lucas coming out of a betting shop together. I waved and shouted but I don't think they could have seen me. I'm glad Mr Lucas is feeling better. Bert

Baxter didn't answer the door. Perhaps he is dead.
   Pandora! You are still on my mind, baby.

Saturday   January 31st

It is nearly February and I have got nobody to send a
Valentine's Day card to.

Witch Week

DIANA WYNNE JONES

Diana Wynne Jones is author of many popular books which are full of magic and often very funny too. *Witch Week* takes place in another world very like this one, where witches develop their powers between the ages of eleven and twelve. This is always a very frightening and unfortunate circumstance, because in this world they burn every witch they can find. Those whose parents have been burnt, or put in prison for helping witches, are sent to Larwood House School. Here they are required to write a journal every day about their inmost feelings. Charles is the only person who does this, but he does it in code. At this point in the story, Charles has put a spell on a boy called Simon.

Nan missed the first manifestation of the Simon says spell. Charles missed it too. Neither of them

discovered how Simon first found out that everything he said came true. Charles left Brian with a thermometer in his mouth, staring cross-eyed at the wall, and trudged back to the quadrangle to find an excited group around Simon. At first, Charles thought that the brightness flaring at Simon's feet was simply the sun shining off a puddle. But it was not. It was a heap of gold coins. People were passing him pennies and stones and dead leaves.

To each thing as he took it, Simon said, 'This is a gold coin. This is another gold coin.' When that got boring he said, 'This is a *rare* gold coin. These are pieces of eight. This is a doubloon . . .'

Charles shoved his way to the front of the crowd and watched, utterly disgusted. Trust Simon to turn things to his own advantage! Gold chinked down on the heap. Simon must have been a millionaire by this time.

With a great clatter of running feet, the girls arrived. Theresa, with her knitting-bag hanging on her arm, pushed her way to the front, beside Charles. She was so astonished at the size of the pile of gold that she crossed the invisible line and spoke to Simon.

'How are you *doing* it, Simon?'

Simon laughed. He was like a drunk person by this time. 'I've got the Golden Touch!' he said. Of course this immediately became the truth. 'Just like that king in the story. Look.' He reached for Theresa's knitting. Theresa indignantly snatched the knitting away and gave Simon a push at the same time. The result was that Simon touched her hand.

The knitting fell on the ground. Theresa screamed, and stood holding her hand out, and then screamed again because her hand was too heavy to hold up. It dropped down against her skirt, a bright golden metal hand, on the end of an ordinary human arm.

Out of the shocked silence which followed, Nirupam said, 'Be very careful what you say, Simon.'

'Why?' said Simon.

'Because everything you say becomes true,' Nirupam said.

Evidently, Simon had not quite seen the extent of his powers. 'You mean,' he said, 'I haven't got the Golden Touch.' Instantly, he hadn't. 'Let's test this,' he said. He bent down and picked up Theresa's knitting. It was still knitting, in a slightly muddy bag.

'Put it down!' Theresa said faintly. 'I shall go to Miss Cadwallader.'

'No you won't,' said Simon, and that was true too. He looked at the knitting and considered. 'This knitting,' he announced, 'is really two little caretaker's dogs.'

The bag began to writhe about in his hands. Simon hurriedly dropped it with a sharp chink, on to the heap of gold. The bag heaved. Little shrill yappings came from inside it, and furious scrabbling. One little white bootee-dog burst out of it, shortly followed by a second. They ran on little minute legs, down the heap of gold and in among people's legs. Everyone got rather quickly out of their way. Everyone turned and watched as the two tiny white dogs went running and running into the distance across the quadrangle.

Theresa started to cry. 'That was my knitting, you beast!'

'So?' Simon said, laughing.

Theresa lifted up her golden hand with her ordinary one and hit him with it. It was stupid of her, because she risked breaking her arm, but it was certainly effective. It nearly knocked Simon out. He sat down heavily on his heap of gold. 'Ow!' said Theresa. 'And I hope that hurt!'

'It didn't,' said Simon, and got up smiling and, of course, unhurt.

Theresa went for him again, double-handed.

Simon skipped aside. 'You haven't got one golden hand,' he said.

There was suddenly space where Theresa's heavy golden hand had been. Her arm ended in a round pink wrist. Theresa stared at it. 'How shall I knit?' she said.

'I mean,' Simon said carefully, 'that you have two ordinary hands.'

Theresa looked at her two perfectly ordinary human hands and burst into strange, artificial-sounding laughter. 'Somebody kill him for me!' she said. 'Quickly!'

Nobody offered to. Everybody was too shattered. Delia took Theresa's arm and led her tenderly away. The bell rang for afternoon lessons as they went.

'This is marvellous fun!' Simon said. 'From now on, I'm all in favour of witchcraft.'

Charles trudged off to lessons, wondering how he could cancel the spell.

Simon arrived late for lessons. He had been making sure his heap of gold was safe. 'I'm sorry, sir,' he said to Mr Crossley. And sorry he was. Tears came into his eyes, he was so sorry.

'That's all right, Simon,' Mr Crossley said kindly, and everyone else felt compelled to look at Simon with deep sympathy.

You can't win with people like Simon, Charles thought bitterly. Anyone else would have been in bad trouble by now. And it was exasperating the way nobody so much as dreamed of accusing Simon of witchcraft. They kept looking at Nan Pilgrim instead.

Nan felt much the same about Theresa. Theresa arrived ten minutes after Simon, very white and sniffing rather. She was led in tenderly by Delia, and received almost as much sympathy as Simon. 'Just gave her an aspirin and sent her away!' Nan heard Delia whisper indignantly to Karen. 'I do think she ought to have been allowed to lie down, after all she's been through!'

What about all *I've* been through? Nan thought. No, it was Theresa's right to be in the right, as much as it was Simon's.

Nan had been given the full story by Estelle. Estelle was always ready to talk in class, and she was particularly ready, now that Karen seemed to have joined

Theresa's friends. She knitted away under her desk at her baby's bonnet, and whispered and whispered. Nor was she the only one. Mr Crossley kept calling for quiet, but the whispers and rustling hardly abated at all. Notes kept arriving on Nan's desk. The first to arrive was from Dan Smith.

Make me the same as Simon and I'll be your friend for ever, it said.

Most of the other notes said the same. All were very respectful. But one note was different. This one said, *Meet me around the back after lessons. I think you need help and I can advise you.* It was not signed. Nan wondered about it. She had seen the writing before, but she did not know whose it was.

She supposed she did need help. She really was a witch now. No one but a witch could fly a broomstick. She knew she was in danger and she knew she should be terrified. But she was not. She felt happy and strong, with a happiness and strength that seemed to be welling up from deep inside her. She kept remembering the way she had started to laugh when the broomstick went flying around the bathroom with herself dangling underneath it, and the way she seemed to understand by instinct what the broom wanted. Hair-raising as it had been, she had enjoyed it thoroughly. It was like coming into her birthright.

'Of course, Simon always said you were a witch,' Estelle whispered.

That reduced Nan's joy a little. There was another witch in 6B, she did not doubt that. And that witch had, for some mad reason, made everything Simon said come true. He must be one of Simon's friends. And it was quite possible that Simon, while he was under the spell, had happened to say that Nan was a witch. So of course she would have become one.

Nan refused to believe it. She *was* a witch. She wanted to be one. She came from a long line of witches, stretching back beyond even Dulcinea Wilkes herself. She felt she had a *right* to be a witch.

All this while, Mr Crossley was trying to give 6B a geography lesson. He had got to the point where he was precious near giving up and giving everyone detention instead. He had one last try. He could see that the unrest was centring on Simon, with a subcentre around Nan, so he tried to make use of it by asking Simon questions.

'Now the geography of Finland is very much affected by the last ice age. Simon, what happens in an ice age?'

Simon dragged his mind away from dreams of gold and glory. 'Everything is very cold,' he said. A blast of cold air swept through the room, making everyone's teeth chatter. 'And goes on getting colder, I suppose,' Simon added unwisely. The air in the room swiftly became icy. 6B's breath rolled out in steam. The windows misted over and froze, almost at once, into frosty patterns. Icicles began to grow under the radiators. Frost whitened the desks.

There was a chorus of shivers and groans, and Nirupam hissed, '*Watch* it!'

'I mean everything gets very hot,' Simon said hastily.

Before Mr Crossley had time to wonder why he was shivering, the cold was replaced by tropical heat. The frost slid away down the windows. The icicles tinkled off the radiators. For an instant, the room seemed fine and warm, until the frozen water evaporated. This produced a thick, steamy fog. In the murk, people were gasping. Some faces turned red, others white, and sweat ran on foreheads, adding to the fog.

Mr Crossley put a hand to his forehead, thinking he might be getting the flu. The room seemed so dim suddenly. 'Some theories do say that an ice age starts with extreme heat,' he said uncertainly.

'But I say everything is normal for this time of year,' Simon said, desperately trying to adjust the temperature.

Instantly it was. The classroom reverted to its usual way of being not quite warm enough, though still a little damp. Mr Crossley found he felt better. 'Stop talking nonsense, Simon!' he said angrily.

Simon, with incredulity, realized that he might get into trouble. He tried to pass the whole thing off in his usual lordly way. 'Well, sir, nobody really knows a thing about ice ages, do they?'

'We'll see about that,' Mr Crossley said grimly.

And of course nobody did. When he came to ask Estelle to describe an ice age, Mr Crossley found himself wondering just why he was asking about something which did not exist. No wonder Estelle looked so blank. He rounded back on Simon. 'Is this a joke of some kind? What are you thinking of?'

'Me? I'm not thinking of anything!' Simon said defensively. With disastrous results.

Ah! This is more like it! Charles thought, watching the look of complete vacancy growing on Simon's face.

Theresa saw Simon's eyes glaze and his jaw drop and jumped to her feet with a scream. 'Stop him!' she screamed. 'Kill him! Do something to him before he says another word!'

'Sit down, Theresa,' said Mr Crossley.

Theresa stayed standing up. 'You wouldn't believe what he's done already!' she shouted. 'And now look at him. If he says a word in that state –'

Mr Crossley looked at Simon. The boy seemed to be pretending to be an idiot now. What was the matter with everyone? 'Take that look off your face, Simon,' he said. 'You're not that much of a fool.'

Simon was now in a state of perfect blankness. And in that state, people have a way of picking up and echoing anything that is said to them. 'Not that much of a fool,' he said slurrily. The vacancy of his face was joined by a look of deep cunning. Perhaps that was just as well, Charles thought. There was no doubt that Theresa had a point.

'Don't *speak* to him!' Theresa shouted. 'Don't you understand? It's every word he says! And –' She swung around and pointed at Nan. 'It's all *her* fault!'

Before lunch, Nan would have quailed in front of

Theresa's pointing finger and everyone's eyes turned on her. But she had ridden a broomstick now, and things were different. She was able to look scornfully at Theresa. 'What nonsense!' she said.

Mr Crossley was forced to agree that Nan was right. 'Don't be ridiculous, Theresa,' he said. 'I told you to sit down.' And he relieved his feelings by giving both Theresa and Simon an hour in detention.

'Detention!' Theresa exclaimed, and sat down with a bump. She was outraged.

Simon, however, uttered a cunning chuckle. 'You think you've got me, don't you?' he said.

'Yes, I do,' said Mr Crossley. 'Make it an hour and a half.'

Simon opened his mouth to say something else. But here Nirupam intervened. He leaned over and whispered to Simon, 'You're very clever. Clever people keep their mouths shut.'

Simon nodded slowly, with immense, stupid wisdom. And, to Charles's disappointment, he seemed to take Nirupam's advice.

'Get your journals out,' Mr Crossley said wearily. There should be some peace now at least, he thought.

People opened their journals. They spread today's page in front of them. They picked up pens. And at that point, even those who had not realized already saw that there was almost nothing they dared write down. It was most frustrating. Here they were, with real, interesting events going on for once, and plenty of things to say, and almost none of it was fit for Miss

Cadwallader's eyes. People chewed pens, shifted, scratched their heads, and stared at the ceiling. The most pitiable ones were those who were planning to ask Nan to endow them with the Golden Touch, or instant fame, or some other good thing. If they described any of the magic Nan was thought to have done, she would be arrested for witchcraft, and they would have killed the goose that laid the golden eggs.

Nan Pilgrim is not really a witch, Dan Smith wrote, after much hard thinking. He had rather a stomach-ache after last night's midnight feast and it made his mind go slow. *I never thought she was really, it was just Mr Crossley having a joke. There was a practical joke this morning, it must have been hard work pinching everyone's shoes like that and then someone pinched my spikes and got me really mad. The caretaker's dog peed* — And there Dan stopped, remembering Miss Cadwallader would read this too. Got quite carried away there, he thought.

No comment again today, Nirupam wrote swiftly. *Someone is riding for a fall. Not that I blame them for this afternoon, but the shoes were silly.* He put down his pen and went to sleep. He had been up half the night eating buns from under the floorboards.

My bed socks were ruined, Theresa complained in her angel writing. *My knitting was destroyed. Today has been awful. I do not want to tell tales and I know Simon Silverson is not in his right mind but someone should do something. Teddy Crossley is useless and unfair and Estelle Green always thinks she knows best but she can't keep her knitting clean. The matron was unfair too. She sent me*

*away with an aspirin and she let Brian Wentworth lie
down and I was really ill. I shall never speak to Nan
Pilgrim again.*

Most people, though they could not attain Theresa's
eloquence, managed to write something in the end.
But three people still sat staring at blank paper. These
were Simon, Charles and Nan.

Simon was very cunning. He was clever. He was
thoroughly suspicious of the whole thing. They were
trying to catch him out somehow. The safest and
cleverest thing was not to commit anything to writing.
He was sure of that. On the other hand, it would not
do to let everyone know how clever he had gone. It
would look peculiar. He ought to write just one thing.
So, after more than half an hour of deep thought, he
wrote: *Doggies*. It took him five minutes. Then he sat
back, confident that he had fooled everyone.

Charles was stumped because he simply had no
code for most of the things which had happened. He
knew he had to write something, but the more he
tried to think, the more difficult it seemed. At one
point, he almost went to sleep like Nirupam. He
pulled himself together. Think! Well, he could not
write *I got up* for a start, because he had almost enjoyed
today. Nor could he write *I didn't get up* because that
made no sense. But he had better mention the shoes,
because everyone else would. And he could talk about
Simon under the code of potatoes. Mr Towers could
get a mention too.

It was nearly time for the bell before Charles sorted

all this out. Hastily he scrawled: *Our shoes all went to play games. I thought about potatoes having hair hanging on a rope. I have games with a bad book.* As Mr Crossley told them to put away their journals, Charles thought of something else and dashed it down. *I shall never be hot again.*

Nan wrote nothing at all. She sat smiling at her empty page, feeling no need to describe anything. When the bell went, as a gesture, she wrote down the date: October 30. Then she shut her journal.

The instant Mr Crossley left the room, Nan was surrounded. 'You got my note?' People clamoured at her. 'Can you make it that whenever I touch a penny it turns to gold? Just pennies.'

'Can you make my hair go like Theresa's?'

'Can you give me three wishes every time I say buttons?'

'I want big muscles like Dan Smith.'

'Can you get us ice-cream for supper?'

'I need good luck for the rest of my life.'

Nan looked over at where Simon sat, hunched up with cunning and darting shrewd, stupid looks at Nirupam, who was sitting watchfully over him. If it was Simon who was responsible, there was no knowing when he would say something to cancel her witch-craft. Nan refused to believe it *was* Simon, but it was silly to make rash promises, whatever had made her a witch.

'There isn't time to work magic now,' she told the clamouring crowd. And when that brought a volley of appeals and groans, she shouted, 'It takes *hours*, don't you understand? You don't only have to mutter spells and brew potions. You have got to go out and pick strange herbs, and say stranger incantations, at dawn and full moon, before you can even begin. And when you've done all that, it doesn't necessarily work right away. Most of the time, you have to fly around and around the smoking herbs all night, chanting sounds of unutterable sweetness, before anything happens at all. Now do you see?' Utter silence greeted this piece of invention. Much encouraged, Nan added, 'Besides, what have any of you done to deserve me going to all that trouble?'

'What indeed?' Mr Wentworth asked, from behind her. 'What exactly is going on here?'

Nan spun around. Mr Wentworth was right in the middle of the room and had probably heard every word. Around her, everyone was slinking back to their seats. 'That was my speech for the school concert, sir,' she said. 'Do you think it's any good?'

'It has possibilities,' said Mr Wentworth. 'But it will need a little more working up to be quite good enough. Maths books out, please.'

Nan sank down into her seat, weak with relief. For one awful moment, she had thought Mr Wentworth might have her arrested.

'I said maths books out, Simon,' Mr Wentworth said. 'Why are you giving me that awful cunning look? Is it such a peculiar thing to ask?'

Simon considered this. Nirupam, and a number of

other people, doubled their legs under their chairs, ready to spring up and gag Simon if necessary. Theresa once more jumped to her feet.

'Mr Wentworth, if he says another word, I'm not staying!'

Unfortunately, this attracted Simon's attention. 'You,' he said to Theresa, 'stink.'

'He seems to have spoken,' said Mr Wentworth. 'Get out and stand in the corridor, Theresa, with a black mark for bad behaviour. Simon can have another, and the rest of us will have a lesson.'

Theresa, redder in the face than anyone had ever seen her, raced for the door. She could not, however, beat the awful smell which rolled off her and filled the room as she ran.

'Pooh!' said Dan Smith.

Somebody kicked him, and everybody looked nervously at Mr Wentworth to see if he could smell it too. But, as often happens to people who smoke a pipe, Mr Wentworth had less than the average sense of smell. It was not for five minutes, during which he had written numerous things on the board and said many more, none of which 6B were in a fit state to attend to, that he said, 'Estelle, put down that grey bag you're knitting and open a window, will you? There's rather a smell in here. Has someone let off a stink bomb?'

Nobody answered. Nirupam resourcefully passed Simon a note, saying, *Say there is no smell in here.*

Simon spelled it out. He considered it carefully,

with his head on one side. He could see there was a trick in it somewhere. So he cunningly decided to say nothing.

Luckily, the open window, though it made the room almost as cold as Simon's ice age, did slowly disperse the smell. But nothing could disperse it from Theresa, who stood in the passage giving out scents of sludge, kippers and old dustbins until the end of afternoon school.

When the bell had rung and Mr Wentworth swept from the room, everyone relaxed with a groan. No one had known what Simon was going to say next. Even Charles had found it a strain. He had to admit that the results of his spell had taken him thoroughly by surprise.

Meanwhile, Delia and Karen, with most of Theresa's main friends, were determined to retrieve Theresa's honour. They surrounded Simon. 'Take that smell off her at once,' Delia said. 'It's not funny. You've been on her all afternoon, Simon Silverson!'

Simon considered them. Nirupam leaped up so quickly that he knocked over his desk, and tried to put his hand over Simon's mouth. But he got there too late. 'You girls,' said Simon, 'all stink.'

The result was almost overpowering. So was the noise the girls made. The only girls who escaped were the lucky few, like Nan, who had already left the room. It was clear something had to be done. Most people were either smelling or choking. And Simon was slowly opening his mouth to say something else.

Nirupam left off trying to pick up his desk and seized hold of Simon by his shoulders. 'You can break this spell,' he said to him. 'You could have stopped it straight away if you had any brain at all. But you would be greedy.'

Simon looked at Nirupam in slow, dawning annoyance. He was being accused of being stupid. Him! He opened his mouth to speak.

'Don't *say* anything!' everyone near him shouted.

Simon gazed around at them, wondering what trick they were up to now. Nirupam shook him. 'Say this after me,' he said. And, when Simon's dull, cunning eyes turned to him, Nirupam said, slowly and loudly, 'Nothing I said this afternoon came true. Go on. Say it.'

'*Say* it!' everyone yelled.

Simon's slow mind was not proof against all this yelling. It gave in. 'Nothing I said this afternoon came true,' he said obediently.

The smell instantly stopped. Presumably everything else was also undone, because Simon at once became his usual self again. He had almost no memory of the afternoon. But he could see Nirupam was taking unheard-of liberties. He looked at Nirupam's hands, one on each of his shoulders, in surprise and annoyance. 'Get off!' he said. 'Take your face away.'

The spell was still working. Nirupam was forced to let go and stand back from Simon. But, as soon as he had, he plunged back again and once more took hold of Simon's shoulders. He stared into Simon's face like a great dark hypnotist. 'Now say,' he said, '"Nothing I say is going to come true in the future."'

Simon protested at this. He had great plans for the future. 'Now, look here!' he said. And of course Nirupam did. He looked at Simon with such intensity that Simon blinked as he went on with his protest. 'But I'll fail every exam I ever ta-a-a-ake –!' His voice faded out into a sort of hoot, as he realized what he had said. For Simon loved passing exams. He collected As and ninety per cents as fervently as he collected honour marks. And what he had just said had stopped all that.

'Exactly,' said Nirupam. 'Now you've *got* to say it. Nothing I say –'

'Oh, all right. Nothing I say is going to come true in the future,' Simon said peevishly.

Nirupam let go of him with a sigh of relief and went back to pick up his desk. Everyone sighed. Charles turned sadly away. Well, it had been good while it lasted.

'What's the matter?' Nirupam asked, catching sight of Charles's doleful face as he stood his desk on its legs again.

'Nothing,' Charles said. 'I – I've got detention.' Then, with a good deal more pleasure, he turned to Simon. 'So have you,' he said.

Simon was scandalized. 'What? I've never had detention all the time I've been at this school!'

It was explained to him that this was untrue. Quite a number of people were surprisingly ready to give

Simon details of how he had rendered himself mindless and gained an hour and a half of detention from Mr Crossley. Simon took it in very bad part and stormed off muttering.

Send Three and Fourpence, We are Going to a Dance

JAN MARK

This story comes from a collection called *Nothing To Be Afraid Of* which Jan Mark set in the pre-television days of the early Fifties. In those days people created their own imaginary world of the sit-com, a world that couldn't be switched off when they'd had enough.

Mike and Ruth Dixon got on well enough, but not so well that they wanted to walk home from school together. Ruth would not have minded, but Mike, who was two classes up, preferred to amble along with his friends so that he usually arrived a long while after Ruth did.

Ruth was leaning out of the kitchen window when he came in through the side gate, kicking a brick.

'I've got a message for you,' said Mike. 'From

school. Miss Middleton wants you to go and see her tomorrow before assembly, and take a dead frog.'

'What's she want *me* to take a dead frog for?' said Ruth. 'She's not my teacher. I haven't got a dead frog.'

'How should I know?' Mike let himself in. 'Where's Mum?'

'Round Mrs Todd's. Did she really say a dead frog? I mean, really say it?'

'Derek told me to tell you. It's nothing to do with me.'

Ruth cried easily. She cried now. 'I bet she never. You're pulling my leg.'

'I'm not, and you'd better do it. She said it was important – Derek said – and you know what a rotten old temper she's got,' said Mike, feelingly.

'But why me? It's not fair.' Ruth leaned her head on the window-sill and wept in earnest. 'Where'm I going to find a dead frog?'

'Well, you can peel them off the road sometimes, when they've been run over. They go all dry and flat, like pressed flowers,' said Mike. He did think it a trifle unreasonable to demand dead frogs from little girls, but Miss Middleton *was* unreasonable. Everyone knew that. 'You could start a pressed frog collection,' he said.

Ruth sniffed fruitily. 'What do you think Miss'll do if I don't get one?'

'She'll go barmy, that's what,' said Mike. 'She's barmy anyway,' he said. 'Nah, don't start howling again. Look, I'll go down the ponds after tea. I know there's frogs there because I saw the spawn, back at Easter.'

'But those frogs are alive. She wants a dead one.'

'I dunno. Perhaps we could get it put to sleep or something, like Mrs Todd's Tibby was. And don't tell Mum. She doesn't like me down the ponds and she won't let us have frogs indoors. Get an old box with a lid and leave it on the rockery, and I'll put old Froggo in it when I come home. *And stop crying!*'

After Mike had gone out Ruth found the box that her summer sandals had come in. She poked air holes in the top and furnished it with damp grass and a tin lid full of water. Then she left it on the rockery with a length of darning wool so that Froggo could be fastened down safely until morning. It was only possible to imagine Froggo alive; all tender and green and saying croak-croak. She could not think of him dead and flat and handed over to Miss Middleton, who definitely must have gone barmy. Perhaps Mike or Derek had been wrong about the dead part. She hoped they had.

She was in the bathroom, getting ready for bed, when Mike came home. He looked round the door and stuck up his thumbs.

'Operation Frog successful. Over and out.'

'Wait. Is he . . . alive?'

'Shhh. Mum's in the hall. Yes.'

'What's he like?'

'Sort of frog-shaped. Look, I've got him; OK? I'm going down now.'

'Is he green?'

'No. More like that pork pie that went mouldy on top. Good night!'

Mike had hidden Froggo's dungeon under the front hedge, so all Ruth had to do next morning was scoop it up as she went out of the gate. Mike had left earlier with his friends, so she paused for a moment to introduce herself. She tapped quietly on the lid. 'Hullo?'

There was no answering cry of croak-croak. Perhaps he *was* dead. Ruth felt a tear coming and raised the lid a fraction at one end. There was a scrabbling noise and at the other end of the box she saw something small and alive, crouching in the grass.

'Poor Froggo,' she whispered through the air holes. 'I won't let her kill you, I promise,' and she continued on her way to school feeling brave and desperate, and ready to protect Froggo's life at the cost of her own.

The school hall was in the middle of the building and classrooms opened off it. Miss Middleton had Class 3 this year, next to the cloakroom. Ruth hung up her blazer, untied the wool from Froggo's box, and went to meet her doom. Miss Middleton was arranging little stones in an aquarium on top of the bookcase, and jerked her head when Ruth knocked, to show that she should come in.

'I got him, Miss,' said Ruth, holding out the shoe box in trembling hands.

'What, dear?' said Miss Middleton, up to her wrists in water-weed.

'Only he's not dead and I won't let you kill him!'

Ruth cried, and swept off the lid with a dramatic flourish. Froggo, who must have been waiting for this, sprung out, towards Miss Middleton, landed with a clammy sound on that vulnerable place between the collar bones, and slithered down inside Miss Middleton's blouse.

Miss Middleton taught Nature Study. She was not afraid of little damp creatures, but she was not expecting Froggo. She gave a squawk of alarm and jumped backwards. The aquarium skidded in the opposite direction; took off; shattered against a desk. The contents broke over Ruth's new sandals in a tidal wave, and Lily the goldfish thrashed about in a shallow puddle on the floor. People came running with mops and dustpans. Lily Fish was taken out by the tail to recover in the cloakroom sink. Froggo was arrested while trying to leave Miss Middleton's blouse through the gap between two buttons, and put back in his box with a weight on top in case he made another dash for freedom.

Ruth, crying harder than she had ever done in her life, was sent to stand outside the Headmaster's room, accused of playing stupid practical jokes; and cruelty to frogs.

Sir looked rather as if he had been laughing, but it seemed unlikely, under the circumstances, and Ruth's eyes were so swollen and tear-filled that she couldn't see clearly. He gave her a few minutes to dry out and then said,

'This isn't like you, Ruth. Whatever possessed you to go throwing frogs at poor Miss Middleton? And poor frog, come to that.'

'She told me to bring her a frog,' said Ruth, stanching another tear at the injustice of it all. 'Only she wanted a dead one, and I couldn't find a dead one, and I couldn't kill Froggo. I won't kill him,' she said, remembering her vow on the way to school.

'Miss Middleton says she did not ask you to bring her a frog, or kill her a frog. She thinks you've been very foolish and unkind,' said Sir, 'and I think you are not telling the truth. Now . . .'

'Mike told me to,' said Ruth.

'Your brother? Oh, come now.'

'He did. He said Miss Middleton wanted me to go to her before assembly with a dead frog and I did, only it wasn't dead and I won't!'

'Ruth! Don't grizzle. No one is going to murder your frog, but we must get this nonsense sorted out.' Sir opened his door and called to a passer-by, 'Tell Michael Dixon that I want to see him at once, in my office.'

Mike arrived, looking wary. He had heard the crash and kept out of the way, but a summons from Sir was not to be ignored.

'Come in, Michael,' said Sir. 'Now, why did you tell your sister that Miss Middleton wanted her to bring a dead frog to school?'

'It wasn't me,' said Mike. 'It was a message from Miss Middleton.'

'Miss Middleton told you?'

'No, Derek Bingham told me. She told him to tell me – I suppose,' said Mike sulkily. He scowled at Ruth. All her fault.

'Then you'd better fetch Derek Bingham here right away. We're going to get to the bottom of this.'

Derek arrived. He too had heard the crash.

'Come in, Derek,' said Sir. 'I understand that you told Michael here some tarradiddle about his sister. You let him think it was a message from Miss Middleton, didn't you?'

'Yes, well . . .' Derek shuffled. 'Miss Middleton didn't tell *me*. She told, er, someone, and they told me.'

'Who was this someone?'

Derek turned all noble and stood up straight and pale. 'I can't remember, Sir.'

'Don't let's have any heroics about sneaking, Derek, or I shall get very *cross*.'

Derek's nobility ebbed rapidly. 'It was Tim Hancock, Sir. He said Miss Middleton wanted Ruth Dixon to bring her a dead dog before assembly.'

'A dead *dog*?'

'Yes, Sir.'

'Didn't you think it a bit strange that Miss Middleton should ask Ruth for a dead dog, Derek?'

'I thought she must have one, Sir.'

'But why should Miss Middleton want it?'

'Well, she does do Nature Study,' said Derek.

'Go and fetch Tim,' said Sir.

Tim had been playing football on the field when the aquarium went down. He came in with an innocent smile which wilted when he saw what was waiting for him.

'Sir?'

'Would you mind repeating the message that you gave Derek yesterday afternoon?'

'I told him Miss Middleton wanted Sue Nixon to bring her a red sock before assembly,' said Tim. 'It was important.'

'Red sock? Sue Nixon?' said Sir. He was beginning to look slightly wild-eyed. 'Who's Sue Nixon? There's no one in this school called Sue Nixon.'

'I don't know any of the girls, Sir,' said Tim.

'Didn't you think a red sock was an odd thing to ask for?'

'I thought she was bats, Sir.'

'Sue Nixon?'

'No, Sir. Miss Middleton, Sir,' said truthful Tim.

Sir raised his eyebrows. 'But why did you tell Derek?'

'I couldn't find anyone else, Sir. It was late.'

'But why Derek?'

'I had to tell someone or I'd have got into trouble,' said Tim virtuously.

'You are in trouble,' said Sir. 'Michael, ask Miss Middleton to step in here for a moment, please.'

Miss Middleton, frog-ridden, looked round the door.

'I'm sorry to bother you again,' said Sir, 'but it

seems. that Tim thinks you told him that one Sue Nixon was to bring you a red sock before assembly.'

'Tim!' said Miss Middleton, very shocked. 'That's a naughty fib. I never told you any such thing.'

'Oh Sir,' said Tim. 'Miss didn't tell me. It was Pauline Bates done that.'

'*Did* that. I think I see Pauline out in the hall,' said Sir. 'In the PT class. Yes? Let's have her in.'

Pauline was very small and very frightened. Sir sat her on his knee and told her not to worry. 'All we want to know,' he said, 'is what you said to Tim yesterday. About Sue Nixon and the dead dog.'

'Red sock, Sir,' said Tim.

'Sorry. Red sock. Well, Pauline?'

Pauline looked as if she might join Ruth in tears. Ruth had just realized that she was no longer involved, and was crying with relief.

'You said Miss Middleton gave you a message for Sue Nixon. What was it?'

'It wasn't Sue Nixon,' said Pauline, damply. 'It was June Nichols. It wasn't Miss Middleton, it was Miss Wimbledon.'

'There *is* no Miss Wimbledon,' said Sir. 'June Nichols, yes. I know June, but Miss Wimbledon . . .?'

'She means Miss Wimpole, Sir,' said Tim. 'The big girls call her Wimbledon 'cause she plays tennis, Sir, in a little skirt.'

'I thought you didn't know any girls,' said Sir. 'What did Miss Wimpole say to you, Pauline?'

'She didn't,' said Pauline. 'It was Moira Thatcher.

She said to tell June Nichols to come and see Miss Whatsit before assembly and bring her bed socks.'

'Then why tell Tim?'

'I couldn't find June. June's in his class.'

'I begin to see daylight,' said Sir. 'Not much, but it's there. All right, Pauline. Go and get Moira, please.'

Moira had recently had a new brace fitted across her front teeth. It caught the light when she opened her mouth.

'Yeth, Thir?'

'Moira, take it slowly, and tell us what the message was about June Nichols.'

Moira took a deep breath and polished the brace with her tongue.

'Well, Thir, Mith Wimpole thaid to thell June to thee her before athembly with her wed fw – thw – thth –'

'Frock?' said Sir. Moira nodded gratefully. 'So why tell Pauline?'

'Pauline liveth up her thtweet, Thir.'

'No I don't,' said Pauline. 'They moved. They got a council house, up the Ridgeway.'

'All right, Moira,' said Sir. 'Just ask Miss Wimpole if she could thp – spare me a minute of her time, please?'

If Miss Wimpole was surprised to find eight people in Sir's office, she didn't show it. As there was no longer room to get inside, she stood at the doorway and waved. Sir waved back. Mike instantly decided that Sir fancied Miss Wimpole.

'Miss Wimpole, I believe you must be the last link in the chain. Am I right in thinking that you wanted June Nichols to see you before assembly, with her red frock?'

'Why, yes,' said Miss Wimpole. 'She's dancing a solo at the end-of-term concert. I wanted her to practise, but she didn't turn up.'

'Thank you,' said Sir. 'One day, when we both have a spare hour or two, I'll tell you why she didn't turn up. As for you lot,' he said, turning to the mob round his desk, 'you seem to have been playing Chinese Whispers without knowing it. You also seem to think that the entire staff is off its head. You may be right. I don't know. Red socks, dead dogs, live frogs – we'll put your friend in the school pond, Ruth. Fetch him at break. And now, someone had better find June Nichols and deliver Miss Wimpole's message.'

'Oh, there's no point, Sir. She couldn't have come anyway,' said Ruth. 'She's got chicken-pox. She hasn't been at school for ages.'

Acknowledgements

The editor and publishers gratefully acknowledge the following for permission to reproduce copyright material in this anthology in the form of complete stories and extracts taken from the following books:

The Bread Bin by Joan Aiken, published by BBC Publications, copyright © Joan Aiken, 1974; *The Young Visiters* by Daisy Ashford, published by Chatto & Windus, copyright © Mrs Margaret Steel and Mary Rose Clare, 1919; 'Daisy Parker's Funerals' by Helen Cresswell from *Bagthorpes V. the World*, published by Faber and Faber Ltd, copyright © Helen Cresswell, 1979; 'William Leads a Better Life' by Richmal C. Ashbee from *William the Conqueror*, published by Macmillan Children's Books, copyright © Richmal Ashbee, 1926, reproduced with permission from Pan Macmillan Children's Books; 'You Don't Look Very Poorly' by Anne Fine from *Crummy Mummy and Me*, published by Marilyn Malin Books in association with André Deutsch Children's Books, copyright © Anne Fine, 1988; *Witch Week* by Diana Wynne Jones, published by Macmillan Children's Books, copyright © Diana Wynne Jones, 1982, reproduced with permission from Pan Macmillan Children's Books; 'The Balaclava Story' from *A Northern Childhood* by George Layton from Sky Books series, published by Longman Group UK Ltd, copyright © George Layton, 1975; 'Send Three and Fourpence, We Are Going to a Dance' by Jan Mark from *Nothing to be Afraid Of*, published by Viking Children's Books, copyright © Jan Mark, 1990; 'The Dog That Bit People' by James Thurber from *My Life and Hard Times*, first published by Harper & Row, copyright © James Thurber, 1933, reproduced with permission from Hamish Hamilton Ltd; *The Secret Diary of Adrian Mole Aged 13¾* by Sue Townsend, published by Methuen London, copyright © Sue Townsend, 1982.